THE GARDEN CLUB MYSTERY

Graham Gordon Landrum
and
Robert Graham Landrum

THE GARDEN CLUB MYSTERY

WHEELER
PUBLISHING, INC.
ROCKLAND, MA

★ AN AMERICAN COMPANY ★

Published in Large Print by arrangement with St. Martin's Press in the United States and Canada

Wheeler Large Print Book Series.

Set in 16 pt Plantin.

Library of Congress Cataloging-in-Publication Data

Landrum, Graham, 1922–
    The Garden Club mystery / Graham Gordon Landrum and Robert Graham Landrum.
        p. (large print) cm.(Wheeler large print book series)
    ISBN 1-56895-642-8 (softcover)
    1. Women detectives—Tennessee—Fiction. 2. Large type books.
I. Title. II. Series
[PS3562.A4775G37 1999]
813'.54—dc21   99-11186
                                                                         CIP

Author's Preface

In the summer of 1995, my father came down to Austin to visit me. We had a great good time. In addition to a book signing, we even got to visit the German Hill Country section of Texas. He did something unusual during that time. He discussed with me at great length how he could construct his latest book. What he wanted to do related to my schoolwork at the time, and I could be one of his "expert" advisers.

A little over a week after he returned to Tennessee, he passed away of a heart attack.

Of course I cannot forget that day. In trying to run around town to prepare to leave, I saw a magnificent double rainbow. The rainbow was God's sign to Noah that the earth would never be destroyed by flood again. As light it is an image focused at infinity, but still reaching into our world. My father's life had a grand finale.

Our family found parts of *The Garden Club Mystery* on several writing tablets. Some chapters were also on the computer. What you see before you are those sections and some material that I have added.

Over the past two years, when I was not completing a graduate degree or looking for a job, I managed to find time to finish the work. I have tried to stay true to my father's intent but have had fun adding in my own bit. Very often his books would have a different ending from the one he thought of at the beginning of the process; thus I did not hesitate to spruce things up in the previously written chapters.

My father enjoyed being an author. He got to give talks and come into contact with all sorts of people. It gave him an opportunity to travel and meet fellow mystery writers. One of these even turned out to be an old school chum of my mother. He always was busy reading fan mail and replied to everyone that he could with a thank you and a bit of promotion for the next book. Most of all, he was pleased his readers could get a few hours of enjoyment out of his efforts.

I do not know if he ever realized it, but the names my father gave his two detectives were the same as those of my sister and me. In a way, Harriet Bushrow and Robert Kelsey have become part of our family. Mrs. Bushrow was first brought in to fill the fourth seat of Helen Delaporte's Pontiac in *The Famous DAR Murder Mystery;* she just took over. Bob Kelsey was brought in as someone my father's age who could be more credible as a detective than a nonagenarian with a cane.

From our family to yours, I hope you enjoy this little arrangement of characters with some thorny mayhem thrown in for good measure.

Robert Graham Landrum
March 20, 1997
San Antonio, Texas

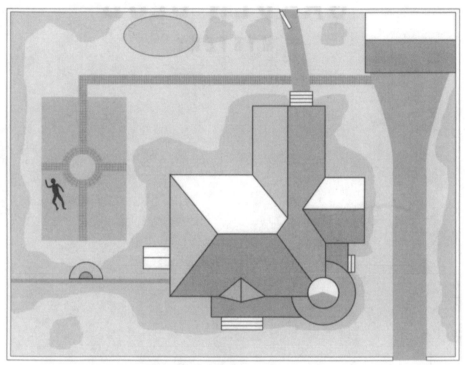

403 Cherry Street, June 6, 1998

Nina's Notes

Notices by Nina Norton

There will be great days in Knoxville for Marguerite Claymore and the four ladies who will accompany her to the Tennessee Garden Club Gala in Knoxville on June 5 and 6. And notice this, ladies: our Marguerite Claymore, known to friends as Rita, will be the honoree at the evening banquet in the grand ballroom of the Regis Hotel. Why? Because it is just 100 years since Rita's grandmother, Mrs. Adam McDurrie, founded the Buena Vista Garden Club, one of the most prominent such clubs in Tennessee. Isn't it marvelous for Rita that she is president of her grandmother's club on this auspicious occasion!

Other ladies who will be going to Knoxville with Rita are Mrs. Arthur T. Wetson, Mrs. James A. Giesley, Mrs. Donald Hythorp, and Mrs. Robert R. Kelsey.

A2 *Borderville Banner-Democrat, June 1, 1998*

Correction

In spite of constant attention to accuracy, errors occasionally appear in our columns. The *Banner-Democrat* is always eagerly willing to correct any false information for which we are responsible.

In "Nina's Notes" by Nina Norton on May 31, the dates of the Garden Club Gala in Knoxville were incorrectly given as June 5 and 6. The correct dates are June 4 and 5.

I

The Corpse in the Garden

BOB KELSEY

It was Saturday morning, the first week in June. Late the previous evening the ladies had got back from their fancy flower show in Knoxville. I don't understand all that I'm told about garden clubs; but my wife, Leota, tells me there are eighteen of them in the two Bordervilles— that's TN 37620 and VA 24201. And when there is a big flower show somewhere or other, perhaps as many as a hundred households in both cities go into a condition of earthquake, tornado, and air attack combined.

Leota belongs to the Buena Vista Club. The girls are awfully proud of that club because it is the oldest on either side of the state line. There are just two ways to get into that high and mighty bunch: you have to be a daughter of a member, or you have to know how to grow flowers. Leota got in by the second route.

That gal can make anything grow. I don't care if it's begonias or petunias or rolmarastrums—she can make it grow. I swear, if she would just plant an old juice can, an aluminum plant would come up.

Anyhow, she has delphiniums that bloom on those long stalks, and I'd say she had fifty to a hundred of them.

Well, Rita Claymore—the kind of woman that has to be commander in chief of any club she may belong to—wanted Leota's delphiniums for a big arrangement she was planning for the showdown at Knoxville; and whatever Rita wants, that's what she gets. So, those delphiniums were one reason why Leota got picked to be among the charmed number that represented the glorious Buena Vista Club at the grand Knoxville show and banquet.

The other reason was the fact that Leota had transportation facilities that none of the other ladies had. That is to say, I have a van; and since I have an obliging nature, I find that I am pretty generally called on by friends and others for hauling things of odd shapes and sizes. That's how I got mixed up in *The Historical Society Murder Mystery,* when Mrs. Delaporte sent me to pick up the portrait of King Louis-Philippe of France that Mrs. Chamberlain had willed to the society. But this time, because Mrs. Claymore was using Leota's delphiniums in her grand "arrangement" and for that reason Leota was invited to go along—but really because the other ladies were going down there in Mrs. Claymore's Lincoln and wouldn't have room for the stuff that would go into the arrangements—Leota had to drive my van down to Knoxville and fetch the residue back home after the show.

I told Leota the club was taking advantage of her. But she said I didn't know what I was talking about, and if I was going to be like that, she would just as soon I would shut up.

The Buena Vista Club received some kind of honor, and Leota was mighty pleased about it when she pulled in home about eleven-thirty Friday night. The banquet had been a big success, and several people had remarked on Leota's delphiniums—wondered how she got them to grow so large and so on.

As a matter of fact, she had the famous "arrangement" in the back of the van and wondered if I would take it to Mrs. Claymore the next morning.

It is amazing how a little thing leads to a big thing—not to say that I realized then that those flowers were the little thing. When I looked in the van that Saturday morning, I had to admit—even if they were beginning to look a little forlorn here and there—those flowers were something to behold. They were in the biggest silver punch bowl I ever saw—property of Rita Claymore—and by the time she got all those spikes of Leota's delphiniums stuck in there along with some kind of ivy and a lot of things I don't even know the names of, my van was just about full of "arrangement." So, after breakfast, about nine-thirty, I lit out in the van with Buena Vista's prize-winning exhibit as a kind of personal backdrop behind me, and off I went to return Mrs. Claymore's creation to her.

Rita Claymore lives in the old family place. It is not quite a mansion, but a big, roomy house, built maybe in the 1890s. Old Adam McDurrie, Rita's grandfather, had the coffin works here. The works burned down years and

5

years ago, but you used to be able to see the chimney and some rusty bits of machinery in a field down by the railroad tracks. Anyhow, the McDurrie family had a nice little sum of money, and their house was what the town had a right to expect of them.

Now we will have to admit that there are bigger houses on Cherry Street alongside Rita's place, but the yard is at least half again as large as anything else along that street. And the yard has always been something to point out as far back as I can remember.

I stopped the van in the driveway, went to the front door, and rang the bell.

I waited and rang again. I couldn't hear the bell.

Thinking that it might be out of order, I opened the screen door and knocked.

"Mrs. Claymore? Mrs. Claymore?" I called. I listened, but there wasn't a sound in the house.

Now, since Rita had told Leota that she would be at home all morning, Leota had not seen fit to call Rita and tell her I was on the way; and I did not want to spend the day hauling Rita's "arrangement" between our house and hers. No way would I have thought of leaving that silver punch bowl on Rita's front porch. No, sir! There has been so much theft and such going on in Borderville, I was going to treat the "arrangement" and that silver tub like registered mail.

So I went back to the driveway, carrying—or trying to carry—that big punch bowl with all those delphiniums sticking out of it. There was water sloshing, too, enough to make the "arrangement" the devil to carry.

The back door was open.

I set down the flowers.

I knocked and hollered.

"Mrs. Claymore? Mrs. Claymore? It's me, Bob Kelsey!"

There was as much going on in that house as you could expect in a country cemetery at six o'clock in the morning.

Thinking that Rita Claymore was on the place somewhere, I decided it would be all right to set the bowl and the flowers just inside the door and go about my business.

I'm afraid I disarranged the arrangement a bit, but you can't expect to carry a thing like that in your arms very far and have it look "apple pie" when you finally set it down.

Then I figured it out. The president of the Garden Club would be in the garden. I would poke myself around the corner, tell Rita what I had done with her bowl, and get to see the place that Leota went on about so much—most of which appeared to be on the other side of the house.

Because what I was about to see is important if you are going to understand what happened, you had better look at the map of the Claymore property that appears facing page 1.

Bordering the side and back of the property is a high board fence with a small gate at the rear, opening to the alley. The fence is painted gray and is almost hidden by the laurel and rhododendron bushes next to it.

There is precious little grass in the yard and only one tree, a weeping willow that hangs over a small fish pond. All the rest is flowers—most of them blooming. I could hear bees humming, and now and then see one dart off for the hive.

I followed the brick walk around the corner of the house and paused there. I couldn't even try to tell the names of all the flowers, but they were everywhere. It just seemed to be all one bed with brick walks running through it. The thought in my mind for a minute was that this woman's thumb was even greener than Leota's.

Then suddenly my attention was caught by something I could not believe. In among those flowers of different colors and different heights lay the body of a woman—face-down.

I went immediately to her, and bending down, called her name:

"Mrs. Claymore! Mrs. Claymore!"

She was wearing faded blue work pants and a tan shirt. She had on old work gloves—leather gloves, the kind that mean business. At the very back of her head there was a nasty gash that had bled enough to mat the hair back there.

But the unusual thing—and the thing the coroner was going to say killed her—was the fact that her face was buried in a pile of very dry, dusty peat moss.

Of course, I turned her over immediately. But there was not the slightest doubt that she was dead and had been so for more than just a few minutes.

As I turned to go back into the house and call the police, I noticed in the flowers just beyond the body a concrete squirrel—a garden knickknack that seemed to have been thrown or used otherwise to cause that wound at the back of Mrs. Claymore's skull.

I went into the house and found the telephone and the police number along with some others on a card taped to the table beside it. (I realized only later that this qualified as an emergency, and I could have used just "911.")

After I put in the call, I went back outside. I didn't mess around with the "crime scene." But it looked to me like I wouldn't be hurting anything if I stayed on the brick walk.

Pretty soon I heard the police car come up, and here came Don Cochran—the detective who had worked on the Historical Society case. He had another officer, a young fellow named Dave Banks. As soon as they saw me, they came and looked at the body. Don had me explain just the things that I have written so far in this chapter.

Banks had his camera and took about twenty pictures from every angle.

"You say you opened the screen door and put something inside?"

"Yes—a silver punch bowl with delphiniums and some other stuff in it," I said.

He didn't seem to be impressed one way or the other.

"Did you touch anything in the house?"

"Only the phone—nothing else. And, of course, the screen door."

He told me to sit in my van until he could finish his work at the crime scene and make a preliminary inspection in the house.

I saw then that he suspected robbery, though I could not see why anybody would try a thing like that in daylight.

By the time I got back to my van and got settled, the neighborhood had found out that the police were at the Claymore place. A second police car had just driven up, and patrolmen were warning a small crowd off the property.

Then a reporter from the *Banner-Democrat* showed up. Someone in the crowd pointed at me. The reporter, a fellow I didn't recognize, came over and began shooting questions at me. He didn't let up until the ambulance arrived and two men carried a stretcher to the side yard. After that, the *Banner-Democrat* lost interest in me and trotted off to get a photo of the corpse being taken away.

In about twenty minutes, Don Cochran came from around the corner of the house and told me to follow him to the police station. There I went over my story again. It was taken down and typed, and I signed it.

By the time I got home, it was almost twelve o'clock. Leota had already heard the news. The telephone lines must have been hot.

She looked at me and shook her head—as though it were my fault.

"Now, you just stay out of this from now on," she warned. "And don't you let Harriet Bushrow get you tangled up in this kind of thing the way she did last time."

10

She was talking about the Historical Society case, when I was in a bad car accident and Mrs. Bushrow might have been killed because I wasn't there when she needed me. But I didn't see how either I or Mrs. Bushrow could have any possible connection with the death of Rita Claymore. And in fact, it was quite some time before I came into the picture again.

Society Matron Murdered

The body of Mrs. Marguerite Claymore, noted horticulturist and society leader, was discovered in the garden of her home, 403 Cherry Street, at ten o'clock Saturday morning by Robert R. Kelsey. Mrs. Claymore had been struck from behind with a concrete garden ornament and was dead when found.

Upon being summoned, the police immediately cordoned off the crime scene. Lt. Don Cochran, the officer in charge of the investigation, refused to release any details.

Kelsey, however, explained that he was attempting to return a silver punch bowl and some flowers to Mrs. Claymore when he found the body. The flowers had been part of a display presented by the Buena Vista Garden Club at an annual convention in Knoxville.

Honored the Previous Evening

Mrs. Claymore, well known for her involvement in the campaign for "A More Beautiful Borderville," had been honoree at the banquet of the Associated Garden Clubs of East Tennessee only the night before her untimely death.

Mrs. Arthur T. Wetson, friend of the dead woman and fellow member of the Buena Vista Club, when contacted by the *Banner-Democrat*, stated that she and others had returned with Mrs. Claymore from Knoxville late Friday night and, when last seen, her friend had been in good health.

"Rita was tired," Wetson reported, "but she was in no way nervous or apprehensive. We are all tremendously shocked."

At press time, police would only confirm that their investigation was ongoing.

Borderville Banner-Democrat, June 7, 1998   A3

OBITUARIES

Marguerite Claymore

Marguerite McDurrie Claymore, 68, of Borderville, Tennessee, died Saturday, June 6, at her home. She was a native of this city and had lived her entire life here. She was a member of First Presbyterian Church, the YWCA, the Wednesday Study Club, the Rebels' Mountain Chapter, NSDAR, and the Buena Vista Garden Club.

Mrs. Claymore will be specially remembered for her efforts for "A More Beautiful Borderville," a program instituted by her in 1982 which has resulted in the planting of over 1,000 flowering shrubs and plants in city parks and in the median of Watauga Avenue. She also is responsible for beautifying the courtyard at the Borderville Public Library.

Mrs. Claymore was the granddaughter of Adam McDurrie, local industrialist, and is survived by one sister, Mrs. Viola McDurrie Coleport; one niece, Mrs. Grace Hannah; and one grand-nephew.

McArens Funeral Home is in charge of arrangements.

II

Investigation of the Death of Mrs. Marguerite McDurrie Claymore

DON COCHRAN

I am writing this at the request of Mr. Robert Kelsey. I have been acquainted with him for many years, having been a member of the same church and knowing him when he worked at the Borderville Post Office. One year ago he was very useful to the police in recovering a stolen portrait of the French king Louis-Philippe valued at above a million dollars and in apprehending the murderer of Mr. Randol Hartwell. In view of his assistance to the force in the past as well as his aid in the present case, the Police Department has permitted me to supply a report of my activities in the matter of the death of Mrs. Marguerite Claymore for inclusion in this book.

Having received Mr. Kelsey's call from the residence of Mrs. Claymore at 10:15 A.M., Sergeant Dave Banks and myself proceeded to the Claymore residence immediately and arrived at approximately 10:25. Mr. Kelsey was the only individual on the premises at that time.

 The deceased was lying face-up in a flower bed on the west side of the residence, the corpse having been turned over by Mr. Kelsey in an effort to ascertain the deceased's condition.

The body was dressed in blue jeans, tan blouse, and sneakers. There were leather work gloves on the hands, and a residue of dusty brown material was evident on the face and upper body. Mr. Kelsey informed me that the material was peat moss, a material used by gardeners as a fertilizer. He assured me that other than turning the body in search of signs of life, he had in no way disturbed anything at the crime scene.

Mr. Kelsey gave me a full and accurate account of his activities in the vicinity of the crime. I directed him to sit in his van while Sergeant Banks and myself continued our examination of the scene.

Death appeared to have been caused by suffocation, occasioned when the deceased, having been knocked unconscious, fell facedown into a small pile of dry peat moss. The weapon with which the deceased appeared to have been attacked was a concrete garden ornament in the shape of a squirrel, weighing approximately eight pounds. This object was lying in a flower bed approximately two feet from the original position of the corpse.

The brick walk was clean and dry, revealing no traces. No footprints other than those of the deceased were discovered in any of the flower beds in the neighborhood of the body.

I instructed Sergeant Banks to photograph the crime scene and directed my attention to the house.

Entering through the open back door, I found myself in a hall running all the way through the house and containing a stairway. To the right, I observed a door leading to a large kitchen. To the left, a door opened on a bedroom. The bed was made and the room was in order except that a garment bag was lying over the back of an armchair by one of the windows and a blue suitcase was setting on a blanket chest at the foot of the bed.

Upon entering the kitchen, I observed a small breakfast table covered with a plastic cloth. This table had been cleared, and one chair was setting beside it.

Opening a dishwasher in the far right corner of the room, I observed a large glass, a juice glass, a plate, a cereal bowl, a cup, a saucer, one table knife, one fork, one spoon, a small skillet, and a bread knife. Inspection of cupboards above the counter adjacent to the dishwasher revealed everyday dishes consistent with those in the washer.

My attention was next directed to a drip-type coffeemaker. About a cup of coffee remained in the receptacle, and the red light adjacent to the switch indicated that the heat was still on.

Beyond the coffeemaker was a bread machine. A small green light indicated that it too was in operation. Calling through the open window, I instructed Sergeant Banks to detail someone to watch this machine in order to get the exact time when the baking cycle was finished.

Then I proceeded through the swing door into a large dining room. The drapes were drawn; and when I opened them, I concluded from the dusty smell of them that the room was not regularly used.

To the side of the swing door was a large, old-fashioned sideboard. The doors on each side were open, and the drawers in the middle had been pulled out and left that way. I concluded immediately that robbery had been the motive behind Mrs. Claymore's death.

There is an amateur thief and a professional. The amateur goes through a desk or a bureau or anything with drawers in it, and nine times out of ten, he will begin with the top drawer. This means that he will have to close that drawer to open the next, and so on until he has opened all the drawers.

Knowing that the longer he is in a residence, the greater the chance of his being caught, the professional thief begins the search for loot by opening the bottom drawer. By leaving each drawer open, he saves time and can be out of the house more quickly.

I therefore concluded that we were dealing with an experienced burglar.

The top drawer of the sideboard was divided into sections like a silver chest, but there was no flatware present. The two lower drawers had contained linens, which had been dumped on the floor. The side doors were open, revealing that these compartments were also empty. I could only conclude that the theft of the deceased's silver had been the cause of her death.

I made an inspection of the rest of the house but found nothing of interest. Based on the fact that the robbery had not been reported upon Mrs. Claymore's return from Knoxville the night before, I assumed that the deceased had got out of bed early, had her breakfast, started her bread machine, and gone into the garden to work when she was surprised by the thief, who knocked her unconscious, proceeded to rob the house, and got away with the silver. Death, I assumed (and was subsequently supported by the coroner's investigation), resulted from the accidental fact that Mrs. Claymore fell into a pile of peat moss and suffocated.

Since Mrs. Claymore was struck from behind, I assumed that the thief wore athletic shoes and thus made no noise on the brick walk; and because the attack occurred on the western side of the house, Mrs. Claymore would have received no warning from her assailant's shadow.

Mrs. Claymore having left the back door open, the thief had no problem entering the house and completing his work.

I was well pleased with my reconstruction of the crime, although one thing troubled me. Professional thieves, and I felt sure that this was a professional, prefer the hours of darkness; and yet there was abundant evidence that this crime had taken place in daylight.

On the other hand, most thefts in the experience of our department here in Borderville are connected with the use of narcotics. If you get one of these users who is hard up for a fix, he is liable to do most anything to satisfy his need as quickly as possible.

After the body had been removed and Sergeant Banks had concluded his photographing and had dusted the dining room for fingerprints, I found the instruction booklet that came with the bread machine. I learned that the cycle of the process took two hours and thirty minutes from start to finish. I explained this to Officer Browning, whom Sergeant Banks had stationed to watch the machine in order to ascertain the time when the process would be over.

About this time Mrs. Viola Coleport, sister of the deceased, arrived. She had been notified of her sister's death by neighbors. It doesn't take long for news about things like murder to circulate in this town.

I explained to Mrs. Coleport that the body had been taken to the hospital, and that when the coroner had completed the autopsy, the body would be released to a funeral director of her choice.

Mrs. Coleport was visibly shaken by her sister's death, but she had her emotions under control and insisted that she would assist my investigation in any way possible.

I took her into the dining room and showed her that the sideboard had been cleaned out. She then described to me what she could remember of the pieces that were missing. These were a full service for twelve in the Edgeworth pattern, a four-branched candlestick about sixteen inches high, two matching single candlesticks, a silver tray approximately twenty-two by thirty inches, a teapot, coffeepot, creamer, and sugar, an ice bucket and tongs, a large loving cup, several bonbon dishes, and a set of twenty-four silver punch cups that went with the punch bowl that had been used in the Knoxville show and was now in the hall next to the kitchen on the floor, where Kelsey had placed it.

That was an awful lot of silver to remove from a house at any one time, especially if taken during daylight. But there it was: if the murder had been done by daylight, it was only logical to assume the theft had been accomplished also by daylight.

I next canvassed the neighborhood for possible witnesses. I had hard luck there. The persons living across the street were on vacation. The neighbors to the east had seen nothing, and the Claymore house was completely obscured from the west by the high board fence and trees in the neighbor's yard.

After an hour's effort, I found only one neighbor who had witnessed anything unusual at the Claymore residence. This was an elderly lady, Mrs. Genelle Tompkins, living across the alley from the Claymore house. Her back fence is a bit less than four feet in height. From her back porch, which is at least three feet above ground level, she can see any person walking through the alley. At approximately nine-thirty, as she regularly does, she came out on the porch to feed a family of five cats, which she keeps in the yard. At that time, she observed a young African-American man exit the Claymore premises through a gate, which he left open behind him.

She claimed to recognize this young man

21

as a frequent employee of the deceased. Though she did not know the boy's name and would not hazard a guess at his height, she nevertheless was certain that she could recognize him if she saw him again. This was the only lead I was able to discover on the morning of the murder.

I returned to the Claymore residence, where I found that the cycle of the bread machine had terminated at 11:45 A.M. Subtracting the cycle of two hours and a half, as indicated by the instruction booklet, I found that Mrs. Claymore had started her machine at 9:15. Mr. Kelsey's arrival at the scene at 10:10 yielded a time of death between 9:15 and 10:10 A.M.

A good number of fingerprints were taken from the sideboard and other parts of the dining room. I felt that in all probability it would not be difficult to learn the identity of the black youth who worked for Mrs. Claymore. I was practically certain that the fingerprints would be his and that the case was practically closed.

I was wrong.

III

The Claymore Feud

HARRIET BUSHROW

Old folks are supposed to be out of it. Yes, I know; and my poor old body agrees. But then, something comes along and reminds me how much fun I had doing such-and-such a thing. That's when I'm like the old fire horse that smells smoke. And the next thing I know, I'm on my hindlegs and raring to go.

So here I am in the middle of this Garden Club murder mystery!

In all my life, I have never been a member of a garden club. There is one rosebush in my yard; it's the only thing out there that blooms. Believe me, it has to do that on its own, for I certainly don't do anything to help it along.

But look at someone like Rita Claymore— such a success in all that beautification and planting around the city. Of course, it was through the Buena Vista Garden Club that she got to be so famous. It's really wonderful what those women did at the various times when Rita was president of that club.

So, it was a shock to see in the *Banner-Democrat* that she had been murdered. But to put a true face on the matter, she was the kind of woman most of us would like to kill at some time or another. I wanted to do it myself once when we were both on the YWCA board one year. But that's not a nice thing to say.

You might wonder how anyone with the personality and disposition of Rita Claymore could be successful with the organizations of this town. We all knew what she was like—from experience or from the reputation she had from people who had had to deal with her. But the truth is that in spite of all that, she will be missed, because there is nobody like her.

You see, Rita Claymore was one of these women who sink their teeth into something and won't let go till they get their way. We may not like such folks, but they do important things for us.

Now, take the YWCA. They had a big old ramshackle house over on the Virginia side—more expense than anything else. If the roof didn't need to be fixed, then the plumbing did; and the next month it would be the wiring.

We had been talking about building a new home for the "Y" for years—while the membership went down and down. Then Rita came on the board and took over.

My, what a change! Before her term came to an end, we were sick to death of her, but we had a new building two-thirds paid for, and the membership was on the rise.

It was the same with every other organization she touched. But it was the Garden Club that she thought was her own property. I'll get to explaining that later; it's enough here to say that she knew absolutely everything about flowers and how to make them grow, and she got behind the women of the Buena Vista Club and the City Council; and the next thing we knew, Borderville was the "beautification queen" of the Holston Valley.

Now, about Rita's obituary...

Obituaries never tell half of the interesting things about the dead. Wasn't it Mark Antony who said, "The good is oft interred with their bones"? Well, it's the other way around with obituaries.

You have to understand a few things about Rita's people, the McDurries. Old Adam McDurrie came here to Borderville more than a hundred years ago.

Borderville is a divided town—half of it in Virginia and half of it in Tennessee—and that makes for a certain amount of complication; those who are Virginians are very proud of it, and those that are Tennesseeans smile at the way the Virginians go on about their state. But when it comes to people from *elsewhere*, well, that just draws us tight together. I should know, because I came from elsewhere (Georgia), and it was a good while before the people here decided I was one of *us*.

As I say, old Adam McDurrie came from Pennsylvania. Not the way most of the ancestors of our people did—in the 1700s—up the Shenandoah Valley, over the divide, and down the Holston. No, he came about 1880— direct—on the train from someplace like Scranton perhaps—from *elsewhere*, don't you see.

And he set up the coffin works that made him his fortune.

Making coffins is not my idea of anything aristocratic, but having money is, and we might as well admit it. No doubt Adam came here instead of some other place because of the convenience of getting hardwoods—walnut and cherry and in those days chestnut—from our wonderful forests. I am sure he made some truly beautiful coffins from those woods.

He had a wife when he came here. Her tombstone is in East Hill Cemetery—a fancy marble column with an urn on top of it and a sort of drapery hanging off. But they had no children. Then, when the first wife died, Adam married one of the Webster girls from here. The Websters didn't have any money, but they owned quite a bit of land.

It was this wife who loved flowers so much and started the Buena Vista Club. Her name was Pearl. I remember her, of course, because she was still living when Lamar and I first moved here. She was a very sweet woman—gave lovely parties and teas—just a gracious, lovely person.

Well, Adam and Pearl had one son, who married and had two girls and a boy: the oldest—Marguerite; then a boy—Richard Webster, named, you see, for Pearl McDurrie's father. The Websters were a Virginia family and highly regarded. And then the last child was Viola. Both parents of these children were killed in an automobile accident. It happened in a terrible ice storm in 1931.

Poor Mrs. McDurrie was left with the responsibility of raising those children. And so it was just God's mercy that she had plenty of money, for she would never have been able to do it otherwise.

Rita and Viola were as different as sisters could be. Rita was cranky and cantankerous—probably took after the McDurrie side; and Viola was just the opposite—sweet and very pretty—though perhaps we would have thought Rita pretty too if her disposition had been better.

I don't know just what happened to the family after 1932, because Lamar and I were in Washington then. (Lamar was an accountant with the RFC until the war and then with the OPA until that was over and we came back here and he worked with Border Electric.)

Maybe it was because Rita was the oldest, or maybe it was because her grandmother by that time was not in very good health, but I really think it was because there was something born into her that made Rita dominate the whole family. Only Richard seemed to rebel.

Neighbors said Mrs. McDurrie toward the last went through hell with Rita and her brother. One story that was told had to do with Richard's pet snake.

I can see how a household of two girls and an old woman might object to Richard's pet; but anybody who has ever raised a boy knows things like snakes come with the terrain.

It seems that Rita—probably with all the provocation in the world—poisoned the snake in some way. After that it was civil war in the McDurrie family, and I must say that my sympathy was with Richard.

Well, the boy was just the right age to be caught by the Korean War. When that was over, he came back for a while and then went out to California and was killed in an explosion of some kind in a plant where he was employed.

Anyhow, when we moved back to Borderville, things were very different in the McDurrie family. The coffin works were long gone—sold to Gaulton, adapted to the furniture business, and then burned after the new furniture plant had opened. Richard McDurrie was gone. That left the two girls. Viola married Irvine Coleport, and Rita was the second wife of George Claymore. He came from Norfolk, and it was said that his family had money at one time—imported coffee from South America—but there was no sign of the fortune when he came here. It was not much of a secret that he married Rita for what she had, which came out of her grandfather's estate.

Anyhow, George is gone—like Richard, perhaps; it was just too difficult to be in the same family with Rita. He just left and didn't come back. Some people said George met with foul play and others that Rita divorced him for desertion; but try as some would, nobody ever knew for sure.

There was a son by George's first wife. His name was Geoffrey, still in his early teens when his father disappeared. He stayed with his stepmother because there was nowhere else to go, and had just one year of college when the Vietnam War came along. He volunteered. He came back to Borderville once or twice; but apparently there was nothing here that would hold him, and we never really knew when he finally cut free. I'm sure it was mutually agreeable to him and his stepmother.

So Rita didn't have what you might call encumbrances in that direction.

The next of kin—the only other possible next of kin—is Viola. Viola is rather quiet; you might almost think she is timid unless you know her pretty well. But growing up with the sister, I suppose she just about had to develop some kind of defense. And the defense she developed was simply to go away when something unpleasant came up and not let it bother her.

I suppose it had been that way all her life, but it came out into the open when the grandmother died.

When old Mrs. McDurrie wrote her will, it was at the end of the Depression. The rather large fortune she left was in securities and a good-size farm. Pearl McDurrie wanted to treat the two granddaughters the same if she could. So she left the securities and the house to Rita and the farm to Viola.

The value of those securities was down among the pennies then because almost nothing paid a dividend in those days. An old house like that in the Depression would have brought something like five thousand. But the farm with a good house on it—that was a living. The silver was the only really valuable thing that Rita got. Viola got the horses—and they were fine ones. I am told old Mr. McDurrie used to race.

So the division was fair enough at that time. But times change; and the value of the securities came back and even multiplied during the war.

Meanwhile, Viola had married Mr. Coleport, who was a fine man and a good husband. He and Viola had a daughter, and they seemed like a very happy family.

But Irvine Coleport had no head for business and ran into debt. They had to sell half of the farm—the most desirable part. And, of course, it takes a lot of experience to make anything from racehorses. The result was that Rita became the rich sister, and Viola was just a poor relation.

It wasn't that Viola held that against her sister. The real cause of the trouble was a cup and saucer. But that can wait.

IV

At It Again

HARRIET BUSHROW

Over the years I have gained the reputation of being a nosy old woman, but now I'm something better: I am a "detective"! If you have read *The Famous DAR Murder Mystery,* you know how it all started. Since then I have solved and written up—with lots of help from some wonderful people—*The Rotary Club Mystery, The Sensational Music Club Mystery,* and *The Historical Society Murder Mystery.*

I'm beginning to think that here in my old age I attract murder and mysteries the way light attracts mosquitoes.

Now, this thing about Rita Claymore: I had no business being mixed up in it at all. I am at the tail end of my life, I just recovered from a broken hip last year, and I've been "poorly" this past winter. But otherwise I've been getting along pretty well for an old widow woman.

I have this dear little Mary Lizabeth Sykes, who was my literacy student. She's the one that works at the little restaurant downtown and helped me some with the Music Club thing. Well, now she's living here at the house and takes the best care of me anybody could ask for—fixes my breakfast before she goes to work (awfully early, but that's all right), two eggs fried, over, bacon, grits with butter

31

melted on top—just what we used to eat when I was young. Of course, that's all the wrong stuff nowadays. But when you're my age, who cares how much cholesterol builds up? People who have old cars don't get upset if they add a few dents now and then.

Mary Lizabeth and I get along like doves in a cote. I've taught her to drive, and she got her license so that she can drive me anywhere I want to go. Not that I couldn't drive, myself, if I wanted to; but Mary Lizabeth is so proud of her driving. I've shown her a little something about how to fix herself up, too, and she's not a bad-looking child at all.

Now, let's get down to who killed Rita Claymore.

It was only a few days after they found poor Rita lying there in her flower bed, and it was ten o'clock in the morning when the phone rang.

I go out on my porch every morning at ten o'clock to see if the postman has put anything in my box. And that day he had—two mail-order catalogs and a circular from the Mountain View Free Will Baptist Church.

I remember that I had the circular in my hand and was reading that the Reverend Alec Boheem was going to speak at the church. The notice explained what wonderful work Mr. Boheem was doing with young boys who are so prone to get into trouble these days.

So I had that on my mind as I hobbled into the house as fast as I could to catch the phone before it stopped ringing.

It was Janet Gaulton, Bill Gaulton's wife,

you know. I was fortunate enough to clear them and their whole family of blame when everyone thought they had had something to do with killing Monica Taybrook a couple of years ago.

She said, "Mrs. Bushrow, we need your help again."

Of course I would do anything in the world for the Gaultons.

She went on: "It's about Slater Watts."

The name didn't mean a thing to me. "Do I know him?"

"In a way. He's one of Lily Dabney's tribe."

Lily worked for years and years for my wonderful friend Iris Gaulton, and I remembered that Lily had this granddaughter who is a teacher in the high school, but I really didn't know the ins and outs of the family. Still, I have always been fond of all the Gaultons, and everyone in that household is dear to me.

"Oh," I said, collecting my wits, "what is the name again—the boy that it's about?"

"Slater Watts," Janet said. "He's Lily's great-grandson."

"Slater," I repeated to get it clear in my head. "How old would he be?"

"Well, he'll be a junior in high school next fall. He's a good student—Janet says he's a whiz with a computer—wants to be a doctor. And naturally Lily is proud as punch over that boy. Isn't that wonderful?"

As Janet explained the problem, Slater had been working—garden work and odd jobs—for Rita Claymore. And when that neighbor across the alley from Rita said she had seen him come through the gate from Rita's yard on the morning she was killed, they took Slater's fingerprints and they matched the prints found in Rita's dining room. The officers hauled the boy down to the police station, questioned him for three hours, then let him go, but they cautioned him not to leave town.

That was bad enough for the boy and his family, but for the great-grandmother—the matriarch and queen bee—it was just terrible.

Poor Lily! None of her folks ever had any trouble like that, and she was so proud of them.

"What can I do for Lily?"

Janet said, "Lily thinks you walk on water and can call off the police."

I didn't see how I could do the one any more than I could do the other. We talked about it for a while; and finally I said, "Tell her I'll talk to the boy and see what I can do."

I went on about my business. Business? I watched a soap opera!

In about two hours, my phone rang. It was Janet again.

"They've arrested him," she said.

"Arrested! Just because he left fingerprints in the place where he worked?"

Considering what I know about Slater's family, I couldn't believe any of them would steal, let alone kill somebody. I knew then I would do anything I could—even walk on water—to prove that poor boy innocent.

"As soon as Bill gets home from Roanoke this afternoon," Janet said, "he'll go down and make Slater's bail."

Lily was always so loyal to the Gaultons; and

though it didn't surprise me, I was just thrilled that the Gaultons were still loyal to her.

"I tell you what I'll do," I said. "After supper, I'll get Mary Lizabeth to drive me over to talk to that boy—find out where he was and what he was doing when the murder took place. Surely there must be some way we can prove he didn't do it. I hope he has a good strong alibi."

Of course, I had no idea what I could do about the situation, but I just couldn't "pass by on the other side." Goodness! I have had to teach that Sunday school lesson too many times for that.

When we got to the boy's house about seven o'clock, I could see people through the screen door. There was the whole Watts family gathered together. Slater's mother came to the door when she saw me come up the walk.

"I'm Mrs. Bushrow. I know your grand-mother and always thought so much of her," I said. "I believe she thought I could do something for young Slater."

The poor woman appeared to be at her wits' end. Nothing hurts quite like some-thing bad that comes to our children. She opened the screen door for me to come in, and I got introduced to the family. I couldn't begin to name and explain them—all the ins and outs and so on—there were so many there, even children five or six years old. I thought: I'll never get everything straight in my head with all these people in this little house.

So I said, "I really think I need to see Slater alone, if it would be all right with you. Couldn't the two of us go out on the porch, or maybe he could sit with me in my car?"

I think the mother saw that I meant business. At any rate, she fetched Slater from somewhere in the back of the house. He probably didn't want all that confusion any more than I did, and I can't imagine that he was particularly eager to see me, a perfect stranger and all. But he came out to the car with me, and we sat in the backseat.

"Now, Slater, I want you to look me straight in the eye and tell me something," I said. "Did you kill Mrs. Claymore?"

His face was troubled, but his eyes were just as steady as could be. "No, ma'am," he answered.

Just like that—no shining, no self-pity— chin and lips just as steady as could be.

"Now that we have that out of the way," I said, "tell me just exactly what you did last Saturday morning."

He went fishing.

"By yourself?"

"Yes, ma'am."

"Where did you fish?"

"At the lake. I went out there on my bicycle right after breakfast. I took a sandwich in a paper bag for lunch. I caught two good-size bass and a crappie. I got home about two o'clock."

"Just what part of the lake was that?"

"I took that dirt road up to the spillway.

There's a path off there where you can get down to the water and there's a nice little cove."

"Did anybody see you?"

"Not down there. There are trees all around."

"And you didn't stop along the way out there?"

"No, ma'am."

"And you carried your bait with you?"

"Yes."

It's a pity he didn't stop in at Darter's store for bait or at least a Coke.

"Did you notice anybody along the road who might have seen you in a way that he would remember?"

"No."

I asked Slater what he was wearing that day. It was tennis shoes, blue jeans, a white T-shirt, and one of those baseball caps half the men around here wear. He said his bicycle was red and white. So you see, there was nothing that would make him noticeable in a way that a person would remember.

I knew then that we might not be able to prove an alibi. And yet, what a wonderful thing—what an American thing—for a boy like that to go off alone, maybe to dream of the future, enjoying the sunshine and the woods and the reflections in the water—just sitting there fishing! I would enjoy that myself. It struck me that Lily's great-grandson must be my kind of boy.

But to get back to business...

I wanted to know all the things the police had asked in their interrogation.

"They asked all about Mrs. Claymore's dining room—what was in it, and what I was doing there."

"And you said?"

"I said I had to go in there to get the silver to polish it."

"And I guess you had to put it back."

"Yes, ma'am."

I thought about it a minute. Of course, that boy would leave fingerprints—coming and going. "I don't suppose you did all that polishing right there in the dining room," I said.

"No, ma'am. I took the silver into the kitchen for that."

Anyhow it might have happened, working there in the house as he did, Slater would leave prints everywhere; and the only witness that could have testified that the boy actually polished the silver as he said he did was Rita Claymore; and she was dead.

"Slater," I said, "I need to know exactly how you went about polishing that silver."

"Mrs. Claymore has this great big sideboard," Slater explained. He used the present tense as if the woman's death was not yet real to him—another thing in his favor.

"There are two big doors on each side," he went on, "with candlesticks and stuff like that inside. All those things were brown and real hard to clean because she doesn't hardly ever use them. Then there is the top drawer. That's for knives and forks and all kinds of spoons and little things.

"And there is a big punch bowl and a real

38

heavy tray. They are too big to go in the sideboard, so they just sit on top. It took most all the afternoon to clean that stuff. Mrs. Claymore is always very particular about anything she has me do for her."

"And I suppose all that beautiful silver was stolen," I said. I didn't know then about the punch bowl and how Rita had used it in Knoxville and Bob Kelsey was returning it to the house when he discovered Rita had been murdered.

But even without counting the punch bowl, that was probably a lot of silver. How would a high school sophomore manage getting all that flatware, candlesticks, and, no doubt, hollow ware bundled up, out of the house, and away? I have heard that thieves mostly put things like that into pillow slips. And yet Rita had been in the house on Saturday night. She would have discovered the burglary if a pillow slip had been taken from her bed or some other disturbance had been made to get a sack. Well, that part of it was strange, and we never did find out just how the burglar got off with such a huge amount of silver.

"Did you touch anything else in the dining room except the two doors of the sideboard and the top drawer?" I asked.

"I might have touched the top of the sideboard. Yeah, I'm pretty sure I touched that."

Of course, the top!

"And you didn't touch anything else?"

"I don't think so."

It seemed to me that Slater's story made

absolute sense. Rita had all that silver. Anyone who has silver knows that we are constantly having to keep it polished, and it is just the kind of chore for a high school boy. I couldn't see why the officers didn't believe it.

I asked: "Other than the fingerprints, was there anything that led the police to think you stole the silver and killed Mrs. Claymore?"

"Well, they had me stand up in a line with some men, and this lady said I was the one—said she saw me coming out of Mrs. Claymore's back gate on Saturday morning. But I didn't do that. I wasn't there."

"Men," he said; not "fellows" or "boys." "Did you know any of these 'men'?"

"Yes, ma'am. One of them goes to our church, and another is on the softball team with Uncle Charlie."

I had satisfied myself that Slater had nothing to do with Rita's death. I told him to try not to worry—just to go back into the house and tell his mother and his grandma and, most of all, his great-grandma that I would go talk to Lieutenant Cochran. You see, I know him because of all that to-do about the Music Club and then the death of Randy Hartwell in the Historical Society thing. You really ought to buy those books, because I wrote in both of them.

Don Cochran tends to shoot at the biggest target around. He sometimes ignores the little things that actually make sense.

40

V

Shot Down

DON COCHRAN

My case against Slater Watts got shot down—but good—on June 10, only two days after I thought I had that case zipped up. But just like that, everything was hanging out.

Lately I have thought I might as well stand in front of City Hall with a sign on my back saying: "Go ahead; throw rocks at me." From about September of last year through August of this year, this area has had the most God-awful series of thefts; and I don't mean small stuff.

There are four jurisdictions involved: Borderville, Tennessee; Borderville, Virginia; Burke County, Tennessee; and Ambrose County, Virginia. Mostly our law enforcement agencies curse this division. It can be a real pain in the you-know-where. But when you have ten burglaries on the Virginia side of town, eight on our side, and so on, you may have a major crime wave, but it doesn't look as bad on the record of any one jurisdiction. Or, at least, that's the way I like to think of it.

But that doesn't change the way the public sees it. And the newspaper! Sometimes it seems that every other story has the headline: "Another Home Burglarized." That word was beginning to get into my dreams and make nightmares of them.

Then there are the editors. They seared our butts all over the editorial page. The public chimed in with red-hot letters, and the paper printed them. The city councils kept jogging the mayors, and the mayor on the Tennessee side kept goosing the Borderville, Tennessee, chief. Then in no more than five minutes the chief would be on my tail.

The Claymore case was the first in which the robbery was connected with a fatality; and, worse than that, the fatality was one of our society people.

We get our share of murder cases—maybe ten or twelve a year—domestic troubles, bar fights, murder-suicide combo. But we don't often see individuals like Mrs. Marguerite Claymore in anything like that. When you get a leading citizen killed on her own property, the public is going to expect action. And if there is a robbery into the bargain, you have to think the thief is the one who did the killing.

Then there were those fingerprints and a witness who not only saw the suspect but knew he worked for Mrs. Claymore. Nothing short of arrest seemed in order.

But I was wrong—not only wrong, but plain dumb. On the morning of June 10, my telephone rang, and when I put the unit to my ear and said, "Detective Lieutenant Cochran speaking," I heard this strong, female voice with a real southern accent: "Lieutenant, this is Mrs. L. Q. C. Lamar Bushrow. I hope you remember me."

How could I forget! In police work, we see all kinds of individuals. But there is nobody like Mrs. L. Q. C. Lamar Bushrow. Good Lord, how can anyone as old as she is operate the way she does? She makes me think of those Mississippi River boats that are advertised on TV—classy and steaming along, not all that fast, but absolutely the way to go. The thing about Mrs. Bushrow that is scary is the way she is nearly always right. That's why I got a sinking feeling when I heard her voice.

She wanted to come down to headquarters and see me at four-thirty, "if that would not be too late." It seemed that she wouldn't have her transportation until then. It wasn't as though I had nothing else to do, but I made noises about how there was nothing I would like better than a chat with her, which would probably go on well past five o'clock, which is when I go off duty.

All right. She came into the office right on the dot. You would not believe how she got herself up to make a call at the police station: great big hat with red flowers on it, fancy beads, white gloves, and all this floating stuff— some kind of material that my wife could name but comes under the heading of information I don't really need—and a gold-headed cane. She could have been the queen of England—not the one now, but that one's mother.

When she came in, I stood up.

I don't often do that. We've got women on the staff and other females that come in and out of my dinky little hangout all the time— in jeans most likely, and a T-shirt that says:

43

"—— Happens." You get out of the habit of standing up when a lady or even a knockout babe comes into the office.

After I got her seated, she began.

"Lieutenant, I am sure you recall that I worked with you before."

How do you like that for starters?

But it is true. There was the Monica Gaulton woman, a real dragon lady if I ever saw one, who showed up dead over at the Presbyterian church. I have to say that Mrs. Bushrow got to the bottom of that case in a way that police procedure knows nothing about.

And then last year there was the Hartwell case, which involved a murder as well as the theft of a picture worth a million dollars. Mrs. Bushrow cracked that one, too, but she almost got herself killed doing it.

"I want to talk to you about Slater Watts," she said. "I believe you made a mistake if you think he killed Rita Claymore."

I threw up my hands. I didn't see how I could have gone wrong about that kid, but I knew I was going to have to defend my lines.

"Now, don't say anything until I make my points," she said, and then she began to lay them out.

Number one was that the only motive suggested for his killing Mrs. Claymore was robbery, and according to her, we did not have evidence that Watts took the silver. Among other things, she pointed out that the boy had only a bicycle and could not have carried off so many large articles on a bicycle without being noticed doing so.

I objected that he could very well have had an accomplice who supplied the transportation.

"Yes, there's that," she conceded, "but until you discover this accomplice, all you have is supposition—no evidence at all."

Then she trotted out her next point, namely, that although Watts is very young, only a rising junior in high school, he would hardly be so stupid as to burglarize a house in broad daylight, as was, she pointed out correctly, my theory.

"True," I had to admit, "but the burglary must have occurred in daylight because Mrs. Claymore was killed between nine-fifteen and ten-ten in the morning." Then I explained about the evidence of the bread machine.

"That was very clever of you, and undoubtedly that was when Rita was killed," she said. "You police officers have to know so much about so many things nowadays. But what I am trying to say is that you assume a connection between the burglary and the murder that does not necessarily exist. And furthermore you are assuming that Slater Watts hit Rita Claymore with that garden thing while he was getting off with the poor woman's silver. But if Slater took the silver, he surely would have done so on the night before. He undoubtedly knew that she was going to be out of town since he was polishing the punch bowl for use in Knoxville. What reason would he have for coming back the next morning to kill Mrs. Claymore?"

"But the burglary has to be the motive for the killing," I objected.

"Why?" She looked at me with ancient but cunningly innocent eyes. When I didn't answer, she went on. "What evidence do you have that a crime that is almost always committed in the dark is the motive for a crime that you know occurred in the middle of the morning?"

"We have the kid's fingerprints on the sideboard," I said. "They prove that Watts was there. And we have a witness who saw him come out of the Claymore property at a time consistent with the victim's death."

"Yes, well," she said, "when you people examine for fingerprints where there's been some crime, don't you have people who live or work at that place put their fingers on one of those little ink pads so you can know which are their prints and which are the intruder's?"

I nodded.

"You know," she continued, "that Slater Watts was employed by Rita Claymore to work in her yard and do things around the house. He says she had him polishing silver the day before she went to Knoxville. Is there anything unlikely about that?"

"No," I said, "not that alone, but the positive eyewitness identification confirms the boy's guilt."

She paused, looking at me with her china-blue eyes—not a look of innocence, but of challenge.

"Who is that witness?" she demanded.

She was really going too far. I was not ready to let that name out.

"Is it Mrs. Terrence Tompkins?"

I didn't say anything.

"As I came here this afternoon," she declared, "I had my driver take me by Mrs. Tompkins's house. I believe she lives directly across the alley from the Claymore place?"

I sighed. "Yes," I admitted. An eyewitness can be solid as a rock or shaky as jelly. But we have to take witnesses as they come. I could see that Mrs. Bushrow was going to find fault with my witness.

Which she did.

"Terry Tompkins—TNT Tompkins—used to play golf with Lamar"—Mrs. Bushrow's late husband—"and Lamar has been dead for thirty years. Terry might have been five or six years younger than Lamar. And then Genelle might have been two or three years younger than Terry. Any way I look at it, I would say that Genelle would be at least eighty years old."

Mrs. Bushrow let that soak in before she added with a smirk, "Poor old thing!"

There it was. I was being challenged as to whether I would believe the evidence of an excitable woman of eighty—and all the while I knew damned well that the woman across the desk from me, by her own arithmetic, had to be at least ninety.

But she was not through with me by any means.

"I suppose you had—I think you call it a lineup?"

I said, "Yes."

"How many were in it?"

"Five."

47

"All black?"

"Yes."

"Lieutenant Cochran," she said, "I wonder if you would describe the men you used in the lineup."

How had I got myself into this? I felt like a little boy standing in front of the desk of a persistent and inquisitive principal. Besides, it was now twenty minutes past five. I was supposed to be at home by this time. But you can't just turn a lady in a big hat and white gloves, with a gold-headed cane, out of your office. I thought of the mayor and the City Council and the paper and all the rest of them that were on my back about our "crime wave." And then, too, there was the race angle.

And what about that? The Tompkins woman had seen a black boy. There was nothing I could do about that. Only now if I had got the wrong black boy—or even if he was the right one and enough people thought I was wrong, all the preachers and bleeding hearts in town would be writing to the *Banner-Democrat* demanding that my hide be nailed to the north wall next winter. If I was lucky, I would be back driving a patrol car.

"I want to know about the lineup," she persisted.

A lineup of blacks is not the easiest thing to get at the Borderville, Tennessee, Police Station. In the first place, we do not have a large black population here in the mountains— never did have. In the second place, unless we have blacks in the lockup, we have to call in two black officers on our force, find the City

48

Hall janitor, and bring in Jake, who runs the concession stand in the courthouse. Then our officers have to get into civilian clothes. And there, with the suspect, we have a lineup of five black males.

Mrs. Bushrow asked very particular questions about each of the fellows in our lineup—how old, what height, weight, etc., and what they were wearing.

"And Slater Watts," she said finally, "what was he wearing?"

"He was wearing a T-shirt, athletic shoes, and a baseball cap." No sooner had I said it than my face must have shown that I had given in.

"Why don't you have another lineup," Mrs. Bushrow suggested, "with young black boys in it—high school boys like Slater? No doubt Genelle saw someone last Saturday, but perhaps it was not Slater Watts."

With that she rose, thanked me for about two minutes, and said she was sure I would get to the bottom of the matter.

When I put up another lineup the following day, using only black high school boys, Mrs. Tompkins couldn't decide between two of the boys. It was one or the other, she was sure; but she just could not say for certain which one it was.

Needless to say, neither of the boys was Slater Watts.

VI

Consequences

DON COCHRAN

I really took it from all sides. The worst of it was the black pastor and the lady Methodist preacher. I tried to tell them I had been attempting to act on the evidence I had. Finally I told them to get out of my office and go to hell.

Instead, along with about twenty of their people, they marched into the City Council meeting, and that's how the racial angle hit the fan and spattered all over the front page, not to mention the editorial page. The only bright spot in my life just then was when somebody tried to get up a mass meeting and only about ten people came.

I was taking it from all sides. The City Council chewed out the chief, who in turn told me if I didn't find something that would please the irate populace PDQ, my job would be hung out to dry and offered as a consolation prize in a charity game of bingo.

Nothing concentrates the mind like the prospect of a man's meal ticket going bye-bye; and my concentrated mind said, Go back to the crime scene and interrogate, interrogate, interrogate.

So I went to the same neighbors I had interrogated on the day Mrs. Claymore's body was found. I made the most careful and complete inquiries, and turned up nothing except that the neighbor to the west, Mrs. Betty Marie Grumberry, had something to add.

She said that when she turned off her TV after watching *The Jane Tittle Show* on Wednesday, June 3, which made it three o'clock, she remembered that she had not mailed the overdue premium to the Bedrock Insurance Company. She immediately went to her garage to drive to the post office. Before she could get in her vehicle, she noticed voices coming from the garden next door.

Although the voices were loud, she could not make out much of what was being said, except that one of them said, "Then you shouldn't have anything to do with money." She was certain that two women were involved, however, and said they sounded pretty angry.

This information threw a new light on the murder. Taken with the point made by Mrs. Bushrow that a connection between the robbery and the murder was not obvious and perhaps not likely, I now had something to work on—a quarrel between two women, a crime of passion. One individual becomes so angry that she picks up the nearest object and hits the other individual with it.

This scenario would have no bearing on the burglary. But if I could just clear up the murder, I could worry about catching the burglar later.

Police Release Suspect

In a surprise move yesterday, Borderville, Tennessee police dropped charges against the suspect apprehended two days ago in the killing of Mrs. Marguerite Claymore.

When asked about yesterday's action, Police Chief Pittson attributed the reversal to false evidence. "The department is processing the case as rapidly as possible in light of the seriousness of the crime and the general public unrest resulting from the recent outbreak of robberies," he stated. "The original arrest was made on the basis of what appeared to be conclusive evidence. But when the evidence went sour, the only thing we could do was to release the suspect."

The name of the involved suspect, who is a juvenile, has not been released.

Borderville Banner-Democrat
June 12, 1998
John Cinic, Editor

EDITORIALS

False Accusation No Answer to Crime Wave

The speedy release of a young teenager from the Borderville, Tennessee jail Thursday is the least restitution that can be made in a situation of this kind. The *Banner-Democrat* congratulates Chief Pittson for the candor of his public admission that the evidence on which the arrest was made was false. On the other hand, the explanation raises serious questions about the efficiency of Chief Pittson's department.

A police department exists for the protection of citizens and their property. The outbreak of repeated robberies—mostly jewelry and silver—which began last summer has been so far undeterred. Public unrest has grown steadily over an eleven-month period and has climaxed with the murder of Mrs. Marguerite Claymore. Mr. Chief of Police, it is time you and other enforcers of the law in this area pooled your resources as this paper suggested two months ago and put a stop to these robberies.

False accusations are a symptom of police inadequacy. If the performance of last week is a true indication of the capacity of the law enforcement agencies along the border, the time for drastic changes in those agencies may be at hand.

The public no longer can put up with shoddy police work of the sort recently displayed in Borderville, Tennessee.

Borderville Banner-Democrat

The High Point of the Mountains   June 16, 1998

Police Department Protested

The Rev. Alec Boheem, Pastor of the Golden Rule Congregation of the True Path Church, led a delegation of his flock into the City Council, Borderville, Tennessee on Monday to protest the recent arrest and incarceration of a young African American on inadequate evidence. The young man involved, who was released last Thursday, was not present as

Rev. Boheem and his followers harangued councilors for 40 minutes before being assured that the persons involved in the infringement of the suspect's civil rights would be censured.

VII

June Meeting of the Buena Vista Garden Club

LEOTA KELSEY

I never in my life wrote anything longer than a letter, and now Bob Kelsey says I have to write up all the things that went on at our club meetings while the trouble about Rita's murder was going on. In my time I have done lots of things for Bob, and it won't be anything new if I do as I have always done and comply with his lordly wishes. So here goes.

The Buena Vista Garden Club has been around since 1896; and from the time it began, the club has never missed a meeting on the third Monday of each month. This past June, the first meeting after Rita was killed was to have been the twelve hundredth time we met. Now, that's a record not many clubs can match, and we didn't take it lightly.

But some of our ladies—Wilma Kilbourn was the main one—thought it wouldn't look right to hold the meeting so soon after Rita's funeral. She called Camille Hythorp, since she's the treasurer, and Camille said that it would be too much. In fact, Wilma called just about every member and talked (to me at least) the better part of an hour.

"I don't see how we can do it," she said in a kind of scandalized voice, "with that tragedy so recent."

She talked about Rita's "passing." Well, I

guess there isn't any easy way to say somebody you actually know was murdered!

But that's Wilma. And all the calling Wilma did stirred up a lot more calling; and, all told, if you could just put the calls end to end, it wouldn't surprise me if our club was on the phone a whole week running. Finally, Frances Elwick—she's a woman of firm ideas anyway—got to our first vice president, Eudora Medborough, who is just the opposite, and told her she would have to put her foot down definitely one way or the other.

Frances pointed out that the yearbook designated the June meeting as the "Centennial Program"; and since Dorothy Weathermore had been researching club history for a whole year (getting most of it from Rita herself), it just wouldn't do to pass up this meeting.

"But what am I going to do to make it right with Wilma?" Eudora wanted to know. "She has said so much about it and all. I just don't know what would be proper."

Then Frances had a great idea: she said, "Why don't we dedicate the program to Rita's memory?"

That did it.

But not before everybody called everybody else again and reported just what each one had said. I wonder now and then how I have time to be in the club and grow flowers, too.

We met at Christine Ashworth's big lovely home out on Mimosa Lane. Albert—that's her husband—is in the bank, and they have just all the money they need. She has this man that works for her two days a week. Her lawn gets more care than most people give their children, not to mention their husbands. But to tell the truth, my phlox and photinias are doing much better than hers; and after all, it was my delphiniums, not Christine's, that Rita wanted for the Knoxville show.

But, oh my goodness! The inside of that house looked like a botanical garden. She is very partial to African violets and had them just everywhere—all in full bloom. I don't know how she manages it. And the baskets of trailing verbina hanging out on the side porch! But she got them from the florist.

When we all had seated ourselves on chairs Christine had rented from the funeral home, Gracie Chidley gave a long eulogy of Rita and all the things she had done—well, not quite all! If Gracie had put in everything, it wouldn't have been exactly what you would call a eulogy, but I'll let that pass.

Then Dorothy got up and gave her program on the club history. Good heavens! That girl really dug into it. Of course, there was a lot about Rita and her family because it was Rita's grandmother who started it all.

As a matter of fact, there were a lot of things in that talk that I never knew before. One thing she said was that *Buena Vista* meant "Beautiful Outlook," and I had always thought it meant "Beautiful Garden." But no, our club didn't start out to be a garden club at all. It was kind of a study club at first—twelve ladies that met once a month in a different home each time. Their purpose was to study anything that would make their outlook more beautiful.

One of the original ladies had a specialty of reciting poems, and they had programs on good books. And then soon after the club was organized, one of the ladies gave a program on "The Language of Flowers." Then one of the ladies gave a program on "The Beauty of the Garden," and by 1905, when garden clubs began to be popular, the Buena Vista Club declared itself a regular garden club.

Between Grace Chidley's eulogy of Rita and Dorothy Weathermore's talk, the meeting came off wonderfully well. Wilma didn't make more than two or three mistakes in the way she presided—which we would hardly have noticed, except that when Wilma is embarrassed it shows so plainly in her face.

At the same time, knowing what we all knew, there was plenty we wanted to discuss among ourselves. We knew that every word any of us might say would get around, and everybody would soon know just what each one had said, but we were saying the kind of thing we would not like to say in a meeting.

So, as soon as we got hold of our cake and our mixed nuts and our coffee punch, we sorted ourselves into little groups; and of all things, it seemed that everybody wanted to talk to me. They all knew pretty much what had happened down in Knoxville. They had heard about it from Gloria Wetson and Pauline Giesley. And now they wanted to hear my view of it.

I have to start by saying that almost all of

the Buena Vista members are rich, and I admit that one or two of the women belong to the club because it is the most prominent garden club in this end of the state and they think it is the one to belong to. Some belong because their mothers and grandmothers did. But the rest of the ladies really just love flowers, though some do more wishing about them than working with them.

Bob says the club takes advantage of me and gives me all the jobs that nobody else wants. Well, yes, I see that as much as Bob does. It just happens that I have always taken pleasure in anything I have been asked to do.

I know it was convenient for the club that I went down to Knoxville in the van and took all the flowers and things the other ladies were going to use in their arrangements and displays, but that doesn't bother me. All the same, you might say that I had come into my own: everybody wanted to hear what I had to say.

As I paused a second or two to decide where to begin my story, Sally Stemphill said, "Oh, come on, Leota. Everybody knows that Pauline is not here today and we know it is because of what happened in Knoxville. So, tell us exactly how it happened."

I explained how Camille and I went in the van with the flowers and so on while Pauline Giesley and Gloria went in the Lincoln with Rita.

Now you must understand two things. Number one, when a member competes in an arranging event—that's arranging flowers for an award—she can use any flowers she wants, no matter whether they came from her own garden, a florist, or the side of the railroad track. She can use any vase or bowl she may like and other objects that might be needed. But—and this is a big but—if it comes out that she had help of any kind putting her arrangement together, she is out; and I do mean o-u-t.

The other thing you have to understand is that Rita Claymore never, never could stand being second to anyone. She will allow someone else to do well so long as she can look good, but she won't let *anyone* get ahead if she can help it. This Garden Gala was going to be *her* show.

I think the reason Rita brought Camille along was to win second place. Camille puts everything into one of her flower pieces. Sometimes she hits the jackpot and sometimes she doesn't. Rita had an idea that Camille would get a payoff this time. Rita also knew who the judges were and that one of them would not like Camille's calla lilies.

I think Camille sensed that she was just there to make Rita look good and resented it a bit. She didn't talk much when we started out. Eventually she got to talking about how she had gotten all new furniture for her whole house.

Pauline, though, is consistently very, very good with her arrangements. In fact, she might as well be professional. She has competed many times in local shows and has a nice collection of ribbons. But she had never had her work in a show as big as the one in Knoxville.

Rita, on the other hand, for years and years had won all sorts of honors in the Knoxville and other shows. She knew that territory, and she was expecting to knock their eyes out with that great big silver punch bowl full of my delphiniums.

I gather that Pauline had told Rita all the things she planned to do for the Knoxville show while they were driving down there. Rita realized that she might have some competition for that coveted first prize.

I happened to be there when Pauline was working on her entry. She had her flowers, and wire, and a shallow greenish-gray bowl, and a few chunks of coral, and was working away. There was this woman standing beside her watching Pauline and talking to her—it just looked like a little comment here and there.

But across the table from Pauline was Rita.

I was still bringing in things from the van, which was why I didn't hear everything that went on. But I did happen to be right there when the woman—the one that was so interested in what Pauline was doing—said, "Now you should put this red flower right there," and she pointed to the place where the flower should go.

As I say, I wasn't there the whole time and don't know what else was said. But it did seem to me that Pauline couldn't keep that woman from talking to her. I only wish I had heard it all, because then I could have told the committee exactly what happened.

Anyhow, Pauline's arrangement was disqualified and it was all Rita's doing, though I don't know just how she managed it. I know it was Rita's doing because after the banquet, Pauline asked if I would be so kind as to let her ride back to Borderville with me in the van instead of going with the others in the Lincoln. By that point Camille didn't mind riding with Rita, so that's how we did it.

That was all I could really tell. But with all that chatter after the meeting, I am sure it got blown up and made quite a story. And it was a dead moral certainty that the facts and the frills added to the facts would be all over Borderville in no time at all. So, with all those women talking about the bust-up between Rita and Pauline, Don Cochran was bound to get wind of it.

I don't know Don Cochran other than that he goes to our church—when he goes, which isn't often—and of course he's the city detective. Bob seems to know him pretty well, and Zena, Don's wife, is a sweet little thing.

Anyhow, Don got the idea that maybe Pauline was the one that hit Rita with that concrete squirrel, or whatever it was.

In a couple of days, he came out to the house and interviewed me—wanted to know all about everything—asked me how Pauline looked when she asked me if she could ride in the van and all sorts of other things.

It was ridiculous.

I said, "Well, surely you don't think Pauline Giesley stole all Rita Claymore's silver?"

"Oh, no," he said. "The theft wasn't connected with Mrs. Claymore's death."

So, you see, he was looking for just any kind of motive. And when you think about it, whoever hit Rita with the squirrel probably didn't think about her falling face-down in the peat moss. And it would be easy for somebody to be mad at Rita enough to pick up the nearest thing and throw it at her. A recent confrontation would be big enough to bring it all about.

I just hated it that suspicion would point to Pauline.

VIII

The Gertrude Morrison Suggs Bible Class

HARRIET BUSHROW

When I got to church on—I guess it was the 14th—the Gertrude Morrison Suggs Bible Class was entirely and completely scandalized. Tongues were clicking sympathetically, and Cora Medford was in an absolute state. It was her story, and she was making the most of it.

Cora was not at all happy. In fact, she was downright indignant. But at the same time, she was enjoying all the attention coming from the other ladies. And I would say that the attention was just about complete.

Cora Medford is Pauline Giesley's mother.

Now, you already know about how Rita did Pauline out of taking a prize at the flower show. Leota Kelsey wrote all about that. And you know that the ladies in the Garden Club chewed over every little morsel of that story. Well, somehow, Don Cochran got wind of that story—it would be difficult to see how he could avoid it—and decided that maybe Pauline had something to do with Rita's being killed. So, if Pauline was a suspect, I don't know what the poor man could do but investigate her.

But Cora didn't see it that way. She was indignant.

"I understand a lieutenant on the police force is not elected," Cora was saying as I came in.

It was a stupid thing to say, but about par for Cora.

"Of course not," I said. "What in the world are you talking about?"

"Oh, Harriet!" Corinna Jones said. She was as dismayed as Cora seemed to be. "Cora says the police think Pauline killed Rita Claymore."

"Grilled her right there in her own living room!" Cora practically threw at me. "Yes, indeed! He actually grilled her."

Oh dear! I thought, poor Don Cochran has his foot in it again. With all the rest of the world—the *Banner-Democrat,* the True Path Church, and the City Council—down on him, he didn't need Pauline's mother and the Gertrude Morrison Suggs Bible Class on his back at the same time.

"But, Cora," Lucile Melloy chimed in, trying to pour a little oil on troubled waters as she usually does, "surely he didn't 'grill' her right there in her own home? Don't they usually take people to the police station to grill them?"

"He grilled her," Cora insisted, "right there in her own living room in her own home!"

At that point I broke in and got Cora to start from the beginning. The long and short of it was that Don Cochran had called Pauline and made an appointment to interview her at her house.

"Now, Cora," I said, when she had reeled off her story and was a little bit cranked down, "that's what the poor man has to do.

It's the way he makes his living. He has to look into every little detail and find out just what happened. That's the only way he can prove that someone is innocent or guilty."

I had to say it over again because Cora doesn't hear half of what is said to her these days—makes up the rest and gets it all wrong, mostly.

"Killed Rita Claymore?" she exploded. "I should say not! She wasn't even speaking to Rita Claymore; so how could she have killed her?"

I got to thinking about that later. Cora was right. People like Pauline don't kill folks they don't like. They just stop speaking. It's the civilized way to go.

Nina's Notes
Notices by Nina Norton

Excitement boils and bubbles in Borderville this week as the Border League prepares for their fund-raiser dance. You'll be able to enter their "Secret Garden" Saturday at the Borderville Country Club. Art Brindle and the Brindle Cats have been secured to furnish that smooth easy-dancing music along with the latest rock and roll. Enid Frothmore, chair-gal of arrangements, tells us that the ballroom will be transformed into a veritable tropical paradise where swains can swing and sway.

This bash will make money for the Borderville Library. Good for you and the other ladies of the League. So, darlings, if you haven't got yours already, get your order on that phone right away because this is one hop nobody wants to miss.

"And what will those lovely children be doing," we asked Enid, "while Dad and Mummy trip the light fantastic?" "Oh, they will be with Grandma." Grandma is the youthful and gracious Kate Logan. Bless you, Kate. What would we do without grandmas?

IX

My Tennis Bracelet and Other Things

ENID FROTHMORE

Fun is fun, and work is work. When I got to bed at 2:30 A.M. after the dance, I wasn't sure that the former was worth the effort and worry of the latter. I mean, I was exhausted. All week long there had been one detail after another hanging in midair. The palms—not real ones—had to be rented from a theatrical equipment company in West Orange, New Jersey. We were getting tropical ferns—real ones—from Knoxville. And a nursery in Parsons City was furnishing hanging baskets of exotics to complete our decorating theme of "The Secret Garden."

Would they all arrive at the same time?

Not on your life. The exotics came on Thursday and had to be hung on the back porch and wherever else we could find a support to suspend them, because there was too much droop to them and we couldn't set them on the floor. The ferns—gigantic things—came on Friday and had to go in our garage. So far so good. But the palms didn't get here until 5:30 Saturday afternoon—two dozen of them.

By that time I was frantic because we could not do a thing about the ballroom until we had the palms.

My committee and their husbands fell to and worked like Trojans. Minivan after minivan laden with ferns and exotic flowers arrived at the club.

Dodo Peterson has this pool thing with a fish that squirts water into it. It is a major production to install—has to have a surround of foliage to disguise the fact that it is just an elliptical plastic tub. And of course the thing has to be filled with water and plugged in at the wall so it can squirt. My Bill, bless his heart, and Dodo's Brent got the thing put together without too much cursing. By the time we had the ballroom in shape, we hardly had time to go home and dress.

Dress! We have to dress in order to have a ball. You've heard of that? Not until the Monday before did I realize that I "didn't have a thing" to wear.

Yes, but it was true. I tried on all the evening dresses I ever owned, and there was something wrong with every one of them.

So, Monday and Tuesday I shopped while I wasn't attending to something else. Finally, I found this darling white dress that would fit perfectly with just the least bit of alteration. It just ought to be perfect against the background of our palms and ferns and Dodo's fountain when they put the spotlight on me and give me applause as "our gracious chair of the arrangements committee."

Wednesday, I took my new dress to be altered. Thursday, I picked it up. And Friday, I went to the bank to get my jewelry out of the box.

So I had all the parts, and it was just a matter of putting them together when I got home from decorating the ballroom. It was already seven-thirty; so I just threw myself together.

When I put on the tennis bracelet Bill gave me when Christopher was born, I decided I needed more color. So I put the tennis bracelet aside and wore my turquoise instead. We flew back to the club—no dinner, just hearty nibbling at the buffet.

I have to say that the ballroom looked really great, and I didn't look so bad myself. And Bill was a darling and didn't drink, so he was the designated driver. When he wasn't dancing with me, he danced with all the old ladies—great for public relations.

All of this leads up to the fact that when we got home, we just fell into bed and it was beddy-bye immediately.

So, Sunday morning—yes, it was still morning—I didn't open my eyes until eleven o'clock.

Bill was still snoozing, but I knew he had a foursome of golf at two, and it was a perfect day for it.

I said, "Bill! It's eleven. Get up."

He sort of went: *"Duhhh."*

I pulled the pillow out from under his head.

Well, so we got ourselves in shape and went to the club for lunch in two cars. We are a real "together." We eat pretty much together and we manage somehow to live in the same house; but it is amazing how often we have to go our separate ways.

You would be surprised at how many of the

terpsichoreans from the night before had lunch at the club that day. Some of them looked a little hungover; and if it hadn't been for the change of clothes, I might have said they had spent the whole night at the club.

After lunch, I picked up the children at Mom's house and brought them home. About halfway to the house, Corey began yelling, "I got to pee; I got to pee!"

Par for the course! So as soon as I got the back door unlocked, Corey was just a blur streaking up the stairs to the children's bathroom.

The toilet hardly flushed when that kid came running to the head of the stairs and yelled: "Hey, Mom, the window's broke. There's glass on the floor and some of it's in the toilet!"

The window broken? You can just bet I zoomed up those stairs almost as fast as my middle one had done. Shandra and Christopher joined the observation team immediately.

"Mom, look there!" Shandra was so afraid that Corey couldn't adequately show me the damage.

The lower sash, which was up—that is, shoved open—was indeed shattered and slivers of glass lay on the floor, in the tub, and, as Corey had announced, in the toilet.

"Well, don't walk all over it!" I yelled. "And for heaven's sake don't cut yourself!"

I'm slow. I know I am. But when things finally click, I come to conclusions fast. This was a break-in. This was a robbery. I flew—and I mean nonstop—into our bedroom and scooted to a halt in front of the vanity.

When I got home from the dance, I had just sort of strewed my things around and didn't put them back in the box—which, you remember, I had taken out of the bank on Friday. Well, the jewelry I had worn at the dance was lying there, but every last thing I had in the way of jewelry had been taken out of the jewel case: my big aquamarine cocktail ring, Granny's pearls, and my tennis bracelet. There is more than four carats of diamonds in that bracelet. Four carats! When you get to four carats, you're talking money.

Of course, there were lots of little things that weren't worth so much except that I loved every one of them. And they were all gone.

The first thing I did was call the club. Fortunately, one of the foursome had not shown up yet.

"What!" Bill yelled.

I told him again, only this time I explained it a little better.

"Don't touch anything," Bill warned. "I'll call the police."

So I didn't touch anything and did my best to keep the kids quiet, and it wasn't long before Sergeant Banks rang the bell. Lieutenant Cochran wasn't far behind; and then Bill drove up.

I explained what had happened.

"Was anything else stolen?" Cochran wanted to know.

I had been so upset over my jewelry, I

hadn't thought about the silver; but when I looked in the dining room, my silver chest was gone, and a cup Bill's father won way back there sometime was missing from the den.

Meanwhile, the kids were like a bagful of kittens.

Sergeant Banks said, "Lady, can you keep them just a little bit still?"

Then Lieutenant Cochran said, "Take 'em outside—no, better: take them to the park so we can get this investigation done before they screw it up."

I gathered up my monkeys, and we went to the playground at the Day School. I am sure all their activity did wonders for their nerves, but it didn't get my mind off my troubles.

After all, there was my best jewelry gone and my flatware, and I didn't know how much it was worth or whether the insurance would cover it. And why didn't the alarm go off? I guess breaking in through an upstairs bathroom window doesn't count against the security system.

I was just sick. It was almost like I had been raped. I didn't think I'd ever feel safe in the house again.

I was just drained. I was a nervous wreck.

X

Investigation of the Frothmore Robbery

DON COCHRAN

I was seated in a lounge chair in my backyard enjoying a cold beer on Sunday, June 21, when the call came. I, in turn, notified Sergeant Banks and proceeded to 1842 Hammon's Chapel Road, residence of Mr. William Frothmore, arriving there shortly after Sergeant Banks. Mr. Frothmore himself arrived shortly.

The Frothmore residence is a large, two-story house with several porches. Because of the rambling nature of the house, with many French doors at the ground level, Mr. Frothmore caused an alarm system to be installed some two years ago. The system malfunctioned several times, and Mr. Frothmore reported that he did not always turn it on when leaving the house. He said, however, that the system had been operative when he left the premises to go to the Country Club at approximately 12:30 P.M. for lunch. Mrs. Frothmore, he said, had returned to the house at approximately 1:45 and found the system still in operation.

A few minutes later, Corey Frothmore, age seven, found a window broken in the upstairs bathroom. Mrs. Frothmore, realizing that there may have been an intruder, examined her jewelry box and found several items missing. Upon this discovery, Mrs. Frothmore notified Mr. Frothmore, who had remained at the club to play golf, and he notified the dispatcher at headquarters.

Search of the house revealed that a number of silver items were also missing. With Mr. Frothmore's help, I investigated the grounds, seeking the method of entry. A branch broken from a tall birch tree near a back porch suggested that the burglar had climbed this tree, thus gaining access to the roof of the porch and from there to the gabled window of a bathroom.

Bark mulch around the bottom of the tree had been disturbed, but no footprints were discernible in the thick growth of the lawn.

Since all members of the Frothmore family had been away from 7:30 P.M. until 2:30 A.M. the previous night, it is assumed that the burglary occurred during that time frame.

Sergeant Banks was unable to find any fingerprints that did not match those of the family.

XI

I Meet the Reverend Alec Boheem

HARRIET BUSHROW

I never—in all my life—did anything for anyone that paid off like helping out in the literacy program.

When I think of the poor folks in today's world who can't read, it just makes me so sad. How can they do anything? Know what street they are on—unless they've been there before? Know the directions for taking their medicine—unless they have taken it before? They can't read a timetable, a menu, a notice from the county tax collector. And heaven knows, even we who can read can't make heads or tails of what the IRS has to say.

How do they ever find out how to get the lid off one of those childproof bottles?

But after you have worked with one of those poor things for a month or so and he reads a whole page for the first time, it is a truly wonderful thing to see that face light up. He is no longer a poor thing.

Anyhow, it was because I was helping with the literacy program that I found my little Mary Lizabeth Sykes. You see, I taught her to read, and it was just like I was teaching my own child.

Then, after I broke my hip and was in that nursing home for such a long time—well, it really wasn't that long, but it seemed like it—that sweet child agreed to come and live with me.

At first I wondered how it was going to be, but it has just been wonderful for the both of us.

Oh, she still has her job at the Cup and Saucer—from seven to about four—and then she does all these things for me. It just makes me feel bad sometimes that the poor child doesn't have enough fun.

So I thought up this little treat for Mary Lizabeth—and for me, too.

We have this old theater—moviehouse—oh, it was built back before the Depression when Lamar and I were living in Borderville the first time. It was very elegant, had a real pipe organ—all theaters had them then, for the silent films, you know. The interior was palatial—the way they liked to make moviehouses in that day.

Well, some young people recently got the idea that it was everybody's civic duty to restore the Apex Theater. And that is just what they did—put it back in a condition that might even be better than it was at the beginning. Pity they can't do something like that to me!

Anyhow, the Apex is all done up in fresh gold and paint that's supposed to match the original colors but is much brighter than the way I recall that place in the old days. But maybe we were harder on the building than folks are today. At least I hope so. I remember one of our mayors back then was a tobacco-chewing gentleman who always ruined the carpet wherever he sat.

Now that the Apex is all flossed up, they use it right frequently for shows; not movies—we're too fine for that now—but concerts and things like that.

I don't suppose it will be any surprise to you that Mary Lizabeth is just crazy about "country and western" music. And I think some of it is right nice myself.

So, when I saw there was going to be this bluegrass concert by Rickey Javits and his Clinch Mountain Boys, I said, "Whoopee, I'm going to give Mary Lizabeth a treat."

Now, you know, the Cup and Saucer is nice enough if you find yourself downtown and you just want a bite—just everyday folks eating there, you see. But next to our new, elegant Apex Theater is a place called K.P. Duty, and it's about as elegant as the Cup and Saucer is ordinary.

They have these chef-type soups at K.P. Duty, and lovely fruit salads and quiche— which is something we never heard of in Borderville until about thirty years ago. And all of that is served just at noon down at K.P. Duty, just the time that Mary Lizabeth is working at the Cup and Saucer. But when there is a show on at the Apex, K.P. Duty is open in the evening an hour or so after the Cup and Saucer closes up. So I thought, eating at K.P. Duty would give Mary Lizabeth a thrill, and then we could go to the concert afterward.

Well, we got down to K.P. Duty, and Mary Lizabeth was just as thrilled as I thought she would be, though most of the things on the menu were words she had never heard before. So I explained what each entree was, and so on.

We were having a good time picking out what we were going to eat when I heard, "Why, Mrs. Bushrow, what a pleasant surprise"—just like that.

I looked up and there was Dr. McDavit, our wonderful, wonderful minister at First Presbyterian. Of course he knew Mary Lizabeth, too, because she's been going to church with me right along since she's been staying at the house—Sunday services and Wednesday night, you see.

"Dr. McDavit," I said, just pleased to see him. He had a gentleman with him. "Where's Mrs. McDavit?"

"She's visiting her brother," he said, "and so I'm on the town. Mrs. Bushrow, I'd like to present the Reverend Alec Boheem. Alec, this is Mrs. Lamar Bushrow, one of our most valued members at First Church." He went on to say a lot of things about me—the kind of thing you have to say to be polite. I just wish half of them were true.

The man with Dr. McDavit was a little on the heavyset side. I'd say he lacked an inch of six feet. He had black, black hair—nicely cut and slicked back—and heavy eyebrows and the most remarkable piercing eyes. He was tan and looked to be an athlete a bit past his prime.

He wasn't wearing a coat; after all, K.P. Duty is elegant but not formal. All the same, this Reverend Boheem—I'd been reading about him here and there in the paper—had on a nice sport shirt and didn't look at all out of place next to Dr. McDavit in his regular suit.

"Are you gentlemen going to the Apex for the concert after your dinner?" I asked. I noticed that this Reverend Boheem was wearing a heavy gold ring—not much the kind of thing you would look for in a minister. I've seen rings that size that were lodge rings, or class rings, but this one had a black onyx the size of a five-cent piece—and set right in the middle of the onyx was a diamond that I would think was between a quarter and half a karat.

"No," Dr. McDavit said. "I suddenly realized that Alec has been in town over a year, and I haven't got around to entertaining him until now. You know Alec has organized a ministry for disadvantaged youth—the Circle of Isedee," I thought he said.

"Oh," I said to the Reverend, "I have been reading about your work. The *Banner-Democrat* has run so many wonderful stories about it. Now just once again, how did you pronounce the name of that circle?"

"Isedee," he said very clearly. "What these young fellows lack is self-esteem. They don't think they can make it in today's world, alas. We give them assurance that they can."

Having lived through the Depression years, I really didn't see that today's world was much worse than yesterday's. I said, "Oh, that is so interesting!" I don't know that I really meant it, because I get appeals from so many charity groups that all say the same thing. But it sounded like the thing I ought to say.

"Yes, indeed," Dr. McDavit observed. "Alec has organized his work on quite a unique plan. He has made Isedee into a poor boys' organization with all the initiation, social life, and fellowship that we would expect from a college fraternity, and with the added uplift of spiritual motivation."

I am afraid that the huge ring with the diamond on the Reverend Alec's finger didn't seem to me quite consistent with the spiritual side of his work.

I said, "I think it is so important to support our young men—I suppose it is just young men that you have in your organization?" From the dark good looks of the Reverend I would have thought he would be very successful in attracting young women. But the thought wasn't really very nice of me.

"Just the other day there was a young man here unjustly accused by the authorities. Fortunately, he had friends who rallied to his aid. Just think if there hadn't been any?"

The way he said it, he left it open for me to assume that he was one of the friends who got Slater Watts out of trouble. Well, what he didn't know wouldn't hurt him. So I just let him go on.

"We are so deeply concerned, Mrs. Bushrow. These disadvantaged boys turn to the only stability they know—street gangs. That's why I originated the Circle of Isedee. It is a gang; but what a difference!"

There was that word again.

"Isedee? Is that some kind of Indian word?" I seemed to remember that there used to be an Order of the Red Man.

"It is a secret word, Mrs. Bushrow. This is

the reason for our success. Like the street gangs, we are a secret organization with passwords, ceremonies, and rituals. We differ from the street gangs in that our goals are the opposite of theirs. Our members get the same peer support that delinquents find in the gangs, but our boys are directed to wholesome activities and purposes."

Just then, the young lady came with our orders; and when I turned to answer something she said, my gold-handled cane, which I had hooked over the back of my chair, came loose and fell on the floor. Reverend Boheem leaned over immediately and picked it up.

Meanwhile, the young lady was setting our different things—entrees and rolls and drinks and all—on the table. I don't suppose that took as much as a minute, but I was looking at what she was doing and not paying attention to the gentlemen for that little time, and when I looked back at Reverend Boheem, he was examining my cane rather carefully.

"This must be an heirloom in your family," he said. "I see it is inscribed, 'To Judge Gardner, presented by the Bar of Gloriosa County, 1885, on the occasion of his retirement from the bench.'" He looked at me as though he expected me to say something.

"Yes," I said, "Judge Gardner was my grandfather." I could tell by the Reverend's interest that he saw well enough that the handle of the cane was real gold, and I am afraid it gave him the idea that I have money.

"And this is your granddaughter, I suppose," he said, looking at Mary Lizabeth.

Dr. McDavit got flustered because he had neglected to mention Mary Lizabeth. Of course, I hadn't mentioned her either. But Dr. McDavit said, "This is Mary Sykes. She is Mrs. Bushrow's companion."

Well, I guess that is what she is. You remember in books a good while ago, we used to read of wealthy old women who had "paid companions"? I think that's the impression Reverend Boheem got, and I knew right then that he was going to hit me up for a contribution.

I explained that I was quite alone in the world—had no relatives at all and that I had had a little problem with a broken hip— Mary Lizabeth had been kind enough to stay with me for a while—just, you know, until I was up to being all by myself again. I certainly didn't want him to get the idea that I could be some kind of angel for his rescue-the-boys "fraternity," as he seemed to think of it.

But the more I talked, the more I knew that he had set his sights on me. He was a master of worming out information—and anyone that can worm information out of me has to be pretty good at it. I was halfway put out with Dr. McDavit for letting it go on. He knows well enough that I don't have any money to give. But, of course, he couldn't say to this Reverend Boheem, "The woman hasn't got a dime."

Then I commenced to see that he had figured out my age; and like so many younger people, he considered that someone as old as

I am couldn't last out the year. He was out to get his "charity" included in my will.

Now, that was a joke on him, for I have no plan whatever for leaving this world in the next year—or even in the next two years. So, if he wanted to cultivate me, expecting to get a fortune when I go to the next world, let him cultivate. It's too bad I won't be around to see how he takes it when he finds he's been disappointed.

XII

The Value of Recycling

HARRIET BUSHROW

Poor Lieutenant Cochran! When I went to his office and calmly upset his apple cart, he was very polite about it; and it is not easy for a man of his age and position to behave as he did.

Then when I read in the *Banner-Democrat* that poor Lieutenant Cochran had another theft to deal with, I felt so sorry for him because, of course, it would only be the next day before the City Council and the mayor and the Chamber of Commerce—not to mention the editorial page letters-to-the-editor—would all be down on the poor fellow like a thousand tons of brick.

People are always ready to criticize public officials for this mistake or that mistake. Folks don't realize that it is hard to get everything right when there is pressure from everywhere to get sudden action. It is easy to criticize, but I won't do it. The time to correct a mistake is when you first see it, and that is exactly what Lieutenant Cochran did.

Now this crime wave—all those folks having their silver and heirloom jewelry stolen and now a murder connected with the robbery— if the two things really are connected!—well, it makes us pretty nervous. Crime waves are supposed to happen in New York and Chicago and San Francisco; but this is Appalachia! We don't think that sort of thing ought to happen around here.

And yet it does and always has happened around here. It is just a little worse now than it has been recently. I'm just sorry that the *Banner-Democrat* snarled so much about poor Lieutenant Cochran's little mistake.

And to think—he was so sure he had the Claymore case all settled when I waltzed in and tore down his house of cards. And he looked so sheepish when he saw I was right.

The last time I got mixed up in one of our little mysteries here in Borderville—they just seem to come along from time to time— I was in the nursing home getting over a broken hip. That took a lot out of me and I keep getting older—thank the Lord, I don't want to stop that. But anyhow I look at it, I ought to sit on the sidelines and crochet or make pot holders or something else, but somehow I can't see myself doing that. Yet here I am, not at all a shut-in—I'll not admit that 'til the day I die. But I don't have the zip I used to have.

All the same, I had gotten interested in the Claymore thing, don't you see? I couldn't let it go.

Like everybody else in Borderville, I take the *Banner-Democrat* and read every word of it, except a good part of the sports pages and all of the financial news. You see, I don't care a thing about stocks or stock cars. But I have to read "Nina's Notes" and the obituaries and the politics—I do enjoy politics. When I was growing up, I heard politics from morning to night.

And I have to keep up with the crime in our area.

We have murders here the same as they do in Philadelphia or New York and so on; not the kind of people I would know, generally— domestic problems in trailer courts, grudge fights that go too far, and all of that. And while it's just as horrible when that kind of thing happens to those people, naturally I'm more interested when somebody is killed that I knew or somebody that people I know knew. We can't help being more concerned about things that are closer to us.

Well, I knew Rita Claymore somewhat, and I knew Lieutenant Cochran, and I knew Slater Watts, or at least some of his family, and so I wanted to follow this Claymore thing.

Like I say, I take the *Banner-Democrat,* and like all good citizens nowadays, I recycle. After I get through with the paper, Mary Lizabeth puts it on the top of the refrigerator. Then, when we get too many plastic bottles and tin cans to keep in a big carton on the back porch, we drive over to the armory, where they have these great huge bins—and that and going to church and the DAR have gotten to be the big events in my life.

I declare, we get to see all degrees of Borderville society at the recycle place.

So, there was a good-size stack of *Banner-Democrats* on top of the refrigerator, and I said to Mary Lizabeth, "Bring them here, and

I'll go through them and make a scrapbook and keep up with this Claymore thing and whatever else comes along."

And that's how I happened to save the clippings that you find now and then in this book.

Well, after I began to go through the different items in the paper, I began to notice a few things that the reader, no doubt, has already seen. But I'll just go over them again so you'll see why I decided I just had to get active in this affair.

All right. If you will look on page 1, you will see that in her "Notes," Nina Norton plainly says that Rita was going to be in Knoxville on June 5 and 6. If you will consult the calendar for these dates, you will find that they are Friday and Saturday.

Anybody could easily find out, if he didn't already know, that Rita lives alone. They would think from reading "Nina's Notes" that there'd be nobody at all in her house on Friday night and at least most of the day on Saturday.

Now look at the next clipping. There you find that Nina was wrong. She probably had the dates right on her calendar, but then surely whoever phoned in the notice was wrong, and the Garden Gala was actually on the weekend. Isn't that what anybody would think? So she made the change.

Then, when the paper came out, every one of those Buena Vista Garden Club ladies read it—everybody wants to see her own name or her club's name in the paper, and that's what they look for if there is a ghost of a chance it will be there.

Don't you just know her phone rang all morning long on the 31st; all those women setting Nina straight about the dates of the Garden Gala! But did she correct it in her "Notes"? Not on your tintype! It showed up on June 1 way down at the bottom of the page, along with other corrections.

"Aha!" said our burglar, who doesn't read corrections a day after the item he got his information from, "this old Mrs. Claymore will be away on Friday night. I can go in and get her silver then because she won't be home until late Saturday or Sunday morning."

And knowing that—or thinking he knows it—he doesn't pay any attention to the light that Rita put on a timer or the fact that there is no mail in the mailbox or paper on the porch, because the neighbor across the street has taken it in. You know that's how it was because a neighbor will do that kind of thing—even for a woman like Rita.

Now look on page 66 of this book. There is Nina again with her "Notes." She says there is going to be a big dance at the Country Club on the night of June 20 and mentions Enid Frothmore as chief cook and bottlewasher. So, the world knows she won't be at home.

But she has children, and there'll be a sitter, and with all that activity—the youngsters and all—it's no time for a robbery.

Besides, these are rich people. Just drive by their house. What do you expect the rich to do?

Well, nowadays, they don't have live-in servants, only day help. And they don't keep any good jewelry at home. It's in the bank, except when they are actually going to wear it. So the crook thinks, "This woman will get her jewelry from the vault on Friday because the bank is closed on Saturday; she'll wear the jewelry on Saturday night. Then she can't put it back in the vault until Monday morning."

So all the thief has to do is hang around the neighborhood Sunday morning until he sees Mr. and Mrs. Frothmore go out taking the children—because that is what people are apt to do during the daylight hours on Sunday. Then, because rich people spend a lot of money on privacy, the thief can get into the back of the Frothmore house unobserved. He knows where to look for the jewelry because what a woman wears to a ball is not the sort of thing a modern girl wears every day. She wears the stuff so rarely that she probably does not have a very secure hiding place outside the bank.

Now, a thief that works along those lines is not a dumbbell. In the end, by thinking the way he does, we ought to be able to catch him.

But how did Rita Claymore's murder work into this? Thieves don't set out to kill people. They only kill people who get in the way. And that was the puzzle, because I couldn't see what Rita could possibly be doing at nine o'clock in the morning that could possibly get in the way of a burglar.

The more I thought about it, the more I

wanted to see the spot where it happened. So what did I do? I called that wonderful Bob Kelsey, the one that saved my life that time when we solved the Historical Society mystery.

XIII

Return to the Scene of the Crime

BOB KELSEY

I remember picking up the phone and hearing this familiar voice. "Mr. Kelsey," she said, "this is a cranky old lady too crippled up to get around very well, and I'm afraid she's going to make a pest of herself."

Although the description was not accurate, I knew who it was. "Why, it's Mrs. Bushrow," I said. "Well, what can I do for you?"

"Well, it's a big, big favor," the voice at the other end of the line warned.

Harriet Bushrow said that since I had found the body, and since she had it in her head to follow this case and see if she could make something out of it, would I be kind enough to show her the grounds?

"You could give me a guided tour, you might say," she concluded.

I said that I would be delighted and would even pick her up to take her to the Claymore house. I would first have to call Viola Coleport to ask permission for us to see the place. Viola said it was fine.

Mrs. Bushrow was a little surprised to see me drive up in Leota's nice new Acura—I guess she had never seen me drive anything else but my van. Anyhow, she got in and oohed and aahed over all the features of the car.

When we got to the Claymore home, I helped her out of the car. I had to treat her like blown glass, she is so delicate; however, she was ready to preside, complete with that regal gold cane.

Mrs. Claymore's flowers were still beautiful, but the place was beginning to miss its owner. The grass was growing and so were the weeds. It made me wonder what the next owner would do with this spectacular garden.

We went around by the back door, and I explained how it was open when I got there that Saturday morning. Then we went around the corner of the house to the west side, where Mrs. Claymore had been working. There was her trowel, since no one had thought to put it away, and there was that pile of peat moss that caused her death. Who would think that something as soft and natural as peat moss would be deadly?

"Now where was the concrete squirrel found?" Mrs. Bushrow asked.

I showed her.

"And I believe you said there was an unexplained footprint. Where was that?"

I showed her the spot, which was by some bushes about fifteen feet from the place where Mrs. Claymore died.

"Now this squirrel," she said, "the thing that hit her, where was it?"

I showed her.

"How big was it?"

"Life-size."

"How much do you suppose it might have weighed?"

"Seven or eight pounds—maybe a little more than a brick."

It did seem an unhandy weapon, but if you suddenly want to hit someone over the head, you have to use whatever is available.

"Why don't we see that footprint again?"

We returned to the big clump of bushes—Leota would know their name, but I don't. They were fifteen or twenty feet from where Mrs. Claymore had fallen, and there was an oval spot among them where the killer must have found his weapon.

You know, anything that is left on the ground long enough leaves its mark. The grass and weeds under it die and turn a light color. It looked as if the killer had been in the bushes when Rita came around the corner of the house and began working in her flower bed. The escape route was cut off; so he sneaked up behind her and hit her with the squirrel. She fell forward into the peat moss, and the fellow went on, not knowing that he had killed her.

I knew the wheels were turning in Mrs. Bushrow's head.

"Mr. Kelsey," she said, "I think we need to know what is inside that clump of bushes."

I said, "Certainly," and began to wade in. Almost immediately I made a discovery. "Why, there's a cellar door back here!"

"A cellar door!" Mrs. Bushrow echoed.

Of course, a house of this period would have had one for bringing in the coal. I suppose most of them have been filled in or just left as they were. Rita, on the other hand—or maybe it was her mother—apparently decided to screen this one with shrubs and incorporate the planting into the design of this little garden nook.

"Let me see," Mrs. Bushrow said, hobbling along as fast as she could.

The pair of doors, hidden as they were, had not been painted for a long time and were in bad shape. They were fastened with a heavy, rusty padlock.

This was a disappointment, because we thought we were going to find that the thief had got into the house through the cellar, yet why else would the man have been in the bushes?

"Mr. Kelsey," my collaborator said, "do you suppose you could get in there and see if those hinges are still in place?"

I crouched down. "By golly, you're right. The screws have been taken out on the far side!"

"Just see if you can lift up that panel enough to get onto the steps."

After not too much effort, I was able to lift the doors. Steps led down to a basement door. The treads were sprinkled with the debris of an undisturbed place that is almost outside. Footprints could be seen in the dirt and old leaves. The secured padlock had caused the police to ignore this passage, but it was another way into the house.

I jumped in to see what I could see.

XIV

The Ground Brings Forth
More Than Flowers

HARRIET BUSHROW

Well, it made quite a bit of noise, but it was plain that this was how the burglar got into the house. Although Bob didn't examine the door at the bottom of the steps, I'm sure it didn't present a very great obstacle to the intruder. And, of course, Rita would not have gone into her basement on that Saturday morning any more than she went into the dining room. And because the back door had been open at the time that Rita was killed, Lieutenant Cochran had assumed the thief had got into the house that way.

But after I pointed out that the silver couldn't have been taken from the house in daylight without its being seen by somebody, surely he would come back to the house to find out how it had been entered on that Friday night.

But then maybe he hadn't done so. I made such a big thing trying to impress him that the burglary and murder were separate things— of course, I was mainly trying to clear that young boy out of suspicion—maybe I made such a thing of it that the lieutenant turned his attention more to the murder angle and forgot to check again on the robbery. After all, the way the burglar got into the house wasn't that important.

And to tell the truth, I had pretty well convinced myself of the thing I was pointing out to Lieutenant Cochran—that the murder and the robbery were separate. But it sure did look like somebody had been into the Claymore house by the cellar door, and it sure did look like somebody that came out that cellar door killed Rita. And the only thing that seemed to be certain was that Rita was killed on Saturday morning, June 6, about nine o'clock.

And Genelle Tompkins had said she saw Slater Watts coming out the back gate of the Claymore property. Well, I knew that wasn't true, because Lieutenant Cochran had now found a man who saw Slater on Highway 412 on his bicycle with his fishing pole and all that. But the same time Genelle had proved in the lineup down at the police station that she couldn't tell one black person from another at all. It was even worth considering the way some of the white kids lie around in the sun—and those tanning parlors—I've seen some of them with skin that looked like shoe leather.

While I was thinking all of this out, poor Mr. Kelsey was just as patient as Job; though, as I read the Bible, Job wasn't all that patient. And while I was thinking, I was poking around in the grass with my cane. That's one advantage of a cane: you can poke with it and stir things around with it.

Well, I was just poking away, and my mind was on Genelle and whether I could believe she had seen anything at all. After all, a murder across your back alley doesn't happen every day. So, when it does happen, you want to make the most of it. Maybe the black boy coming out of Rita's back gate was nothing but Genelle's imagination.

All these jumbled ideas and questions were just teeming in my head, when suddenly I realized that my poking had turned something up—something small but shiny. It appeared to be about an inch long.

"Mr. Kelsey," I said. "Do you see what my cane is pointing to? Would you pick it up for me, please?"

He laid it in my hand. It was a kind of pin—brass. It was shaped like this:

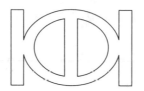

This is the actual size of it. I laid it on the paper and traced the edges of it.

"Did you ever see anything like this?" I asked.

Bob Kelsey looked at it, squinted at it. Held it this way and that. There was a pin and a catch—not a safety catch, but the kind of catch you find on the cheapest costume jewelry.

"Well, I don't know," he said. "It has sort of the shape of a buckle on a lady's belt."

It did look a little like a buckle. Pinned on a ribbon at the right width, I suppose, it would probably look a good deal like a buckle. But who is so crazy about buckles that she would pin something that looks like a buckle on a ribbon?

"Could it be some kind of symbol?" I asked. "A lodge? Some kind of secret order?"

Bob went through as many of the secret organizations as came to mind: Masons? Knights of Pythias? Woodmen of the World? IOOF? No. Finally he said, "Maybe it's a college fraternity."

Now Lamar Junior pledged Phi Kappa Psi when he was in college just before he went into the army in World War II, so I knew what a phi looks like. And the middle part of the pin was just a little like the Greek letter phi.

And then there was the question whether the pin had anything to do with the robbery or Rita's death.

The cellar door off its hinges and the little brass trinket were all that we found, and in a way they seemed to make things more difficult.

That sweet man Bob Kelsey drove me back home and left the strange little pin with me. But when all was said and done, our discoveries had to do with the "crime scene," as Lieutenant Cochran calls it. Therefore, as soon as Mary Lizabeth got home from the Cup and Saucer at four the following afternoon, I had her drive me down to the police station and gave it to him.

XV

Win Some, Lose Some

DON COCHRAN

L. Q. C. Lamar Bushrow—if that isn't a name! And it might as well be Mack Truck, the way she rolls over me. After she gets me flat, she picks me up, dusts me off, turns on all the sugar and sunshine, and leaves me wondering what happened to me.

She came in here along about the last of June, had been over to the Claymore house and was going to set me straight again. And did she ever! All she did was find the intruder's place of entry, prove that it was some twenty feet from the murder site, and convince me that what I knew had happened couldn't possibly have happened!

Oh, yes, she had this little brass pin. Sure, it was found on the crime scene. *I* didn't know what the damn thing was. But she seemed to think I ought to find out.

I never see that lady when she doesn't turn my ideas completely upside down. Here a few weeks before she left me convinced the murder and the robbery were not connected. She absolutely tore down the testimony of my only witness, and now she thought there might be something to it after all. Dave, that's my sergeant, couldn't understand why I even listened to "that old lady."

I listened, all right; but in the meantime I

had heard something that caused me to look at the case a little differently. What I heard was that a Claymore will was never found.

Rumor had it that Marguerite Claymore and her sister spat like two tomcats when they saw each other, and the general opinion in town was that the Claymore money would go to Giles College. At least Giles College had courted Claymore with that in view, but when the will did not show up and no evidence was found that there ever had ever been any will at all, that left the sister, Mrs. Viola Coleport, in big-time luck. When a rich party kicks off in an unexplained way, we always ask who's to profit.

So Sergeant Banks and I interrogated Mrs. Coleport at her home on Monday, June 29. She was cooperative and even served us coffee. What follows is the transcript of the interview.

COCHRAN: This interrogation is taking place at 709 Blanchard Hills Drive on June 29, 1998. Present are Lt. Donald R. Cochran, Sgt. D. B. Banks, and Mrs. Viola Coleport.

Mrs. Coleport, you understand that this interrogation is related to the murder of your sister, Mrs. Marguerite Claymore?

COLEPORT: I do.

COCHRAN: You understand that you have the right for an attorney to be present, and have waived that right. Is that correct?

COLEPORT: It is.

COCHRAN: You understand that you may

remain silent, but anything you say may be used in evidence against you?

COLEPORT: I do.

COCHRAN: Mrs. Coleport, before this interrogation begins, I want to state that the Police Department appreciates your cooperation and that all questions directed to you are for information only and do not imply any malfeasance on your part.

COLEPORT: I understand.

COCHRAN: What was your kinship to Mrs. Claymore?

COLEPORT: We were sisters.

COCHRAN: Would you say that your relations with your sister were good?

COLEPORT: They were not.

COCHRAN: Would you explain?

COLEPORT: My sister was always difficult—from the time we were children. She was jealous—felt that our parents favored me, which was not true. Our parents were always fair in their treatment of my sister and me and my brother.

COCHRAN: Is your brother living?

COLEPORT: No.

COCHRAN: A conversation between you and your sister at your sister's residence was overheard the week before her death. Would you tell us the nature of that conversation?

COLEPORT: I had gone to my sister for financial help. She refused to help me.

COCHRAN: Our information tells us voices were raised. Do you have anything to say about that?

COLEPORT: Lt. Cochran, the whole story of the estrangement between me and my sister is absolutely ridiculous, but you might as well hear the whole thing.

As I said, my sister was always jealous of me and afraid our parents favored me over her. They did not. When our mother's estate was settled, the division between my sister and myself was as equal as a division of that kind can be made. Rita got the house in town and most of the furniture, though there were certain things that Mother thought that I should have—like the furniture in the room that had been mine. I received the farm, with a very livable house in good repair. Cash and stock were equally divided and the timber was divided in the same way. As a matter of fact, coal was discovered on a tract of Rita's woods.

The thing that divided us was a cup and saucer that had belonged to Mr. Thomas Jefferson. Our great-great-grandmother on our mother's side was a friend of Martha Jefferson Randolph and had visited Monticello. As a memento of that visit, Mr. Jefferson gave her the cup and saucer from which she drank tea on the morning when she left for home.

As you can imagine, that cup and saucer was treasured by my mother's family and came at length to my great-aunt, Bea. Aunt Bea was such a sweet old thing and I dearly loved her. She must have loved me just as much because she left the Jefferson cup and saucer to me.

Rita was furious. She thought because she was the oldest child in the family she should have it. Our division dates from the day Aunt Bea died. Rita tried many times to get me to give her the cup and saucer. Each time I refused, there would be a year, perhaps, when she would not speak to me. It could be very embarrassing, because, you see, we both belonged to the Buena Vista Garden Club, founded by our good mother.

Rita has been president of it several times. And once I was president. Oh, I tell you, we have some rocky times in that club.

As I say, I have had some serious financial problems. On that day, I went to ask for a loan of $5,000—the purpose of the loan doesn't matter. I offered to pay whatever interest Rita might want. But she was not interested in that. She wanted the cup and saucer.

As I look back on it, I wish I could have given it to her. I valued it, not because of Mr. Jefferson, but because of Aunt Bea. But I couldn't give it to her, because, about ten years ago, I lost my balance off of a kitchen chair I was using to adjust the drapes in my living room—we were living on the farm at the time. I fell against the table, knocking it over; and the cup and saucer, which was on the table, was broken into a hundred pieces.

I never told Rita—even when she demanded the cup and saucer in return for the loan. I was afraid to. But the way she carried on, it just came over me: I had taken that sort of thing from her for so long that I am sure my voice was plenty loud enough to be heard by Mrs. Grumberry. It was Mrs. Grumberry, wasn't it?

COCHRAN: I cannot divulge that information.

COLEPORT: Oh, I know it was! Well, that's the story of our falling out before Rita died. I'm sorry it had to be that way.

COCHRAN: After the conversation you had with her in her yard, did you see your sister alive?

COLEPORT: The next time was at the funeral home, when I went to take her clothes to Mr. Harcomb and select the casket.

COCHRAN: Are you aware that the silver stolen from Mrs. Claymore's house would have a value something in excess of $5,000?

COLEPORT: Lt. Cochran, I resent the implication. Not only would I never steal anything from anybody; I would not even know how to go about it. I wouldn't even know whom to ask to find out.

COCHRAN: You stated that your mother in her will divided the family property equally. Did this apply to the silver as well?

COLEPORT: Oh, most of the silver that was stolen did not belong to Rita.

COCHRAN: Did not belong to Rita?

COLEPORT: No, that was Claymore silver. It had been in her mother-in-law's family. It belonged to Geoffrey, Rita's stepson.

COCHRAN: Could you give us some information on Geoffrey?

COLEPORT: Geof was George's son by his

106

first marriage. He was seven when Rita married George. He was fourteen when George left Rita. Since Geof didn't have any other relative—any close relatives, that is—there was nothing Rita could do but keep Geof at the house. But when Geof was eighteen, she gave him $1,000 and told him he was on his own. That's how Rita was.

COCHRAN: Do you know where this Geoffrey—Geoffrey Claymore—where he is now?

COLEPORT: Well, yes. You see I liked the boy; and on those occasions when Rita and I were on speaking terms, she taught him to call me "Aunt Vi." I offered him a room on the farm when Rita kicked him out, but he went into the army. He was in Desert Storm. After he was discharged, he began to have mental problems. He is at the Veterans' Hospital in Parsons City.

[Here is where a light went on in my head. I'll go into that later.]

COCHRAN: Mrs. Coleport, you say some of that silver that was stolen belonged to this Geoffrey?

COLEPORT: Yes. The flat silver was Rita's—engraved with Grandmother's initials, since she's the one who originally had it—but the candlesticks and the tea service and a few other things were Geoffrey's, left to him by his grandmother Claymore. She died a few years after Rita and George were married. I guess she didn't want her silver to fall into Rita's hands—though that is what happened in the end.

COCHRAN: Mrs. Coleport, there was a silver punch bowl used for flowers that Bob Kelsey was returning when he discovered Mrs. Claymore's body. Did that belong to this stepson?

COLEPORT: No. That was in my family. Grandmother left Rita her flat silver and the punch bowl. I got Grandmother's tea service.

COCHRAN: That's very interesting. Now there's one other thing. Is there anyone other than you who stands to inherit if there is no will?

COLEPORT: Oh yes.

COCHRAN: There is? Who?

COLEPORT: Why, George Claymore.

COCHRAN: George Claymore?

COLEPORT: Yes, Rita's husband.

COCHRAN: But they were divorced.

COLEPORT: Not that I ever heard of.

COCHRAN: My information was that Mrs. Claymore was divorced.

COLEPORT: You would think she would have divorced him—it certainly was desertion. He has been gone so long, she could have had him declared dead. Divorced or widowed—few people would have the nerve to ask for particulars. But as long as Geof stayed with Rita, his father kept up with him through me. No, George was out in Texas the last I heard of.

COCHRAN: Well, thank you very much for your information.

The interrogation of Mrs. Viola Coleport gave me a lot to think about—namely, two suspects with first-rate motives. The first was the husband. All he had to do was return from the grave and claim his late wife's estate. And then there was this Geoffrey Claymore, who was supposed to be in the funny ward at the V.A. Hospital just twenty miles away. It was his silver—more or less—that was taken. Oh, there was the flat silver, as well; but the man was mixed up in the head, so he could have taken the flat silver, too. What did that amount to? And there he was in the house for how many years? Viola Coleport said from seven to eighteen. Well, now, that kid knew all about the cellar steps.

He was turning into a peach of a suspect, and I could check him out real easy.

Which I did as soon as I got back to my office—a simple telephone call. Geoffrey Thomas Claymore, honorably discharged sergeant major, had been treated for mild paranoia and released only two months prior to the burglary and murder of Mrs. Marguerite McDurrie Claymore. They gave me his forwarding address—a little town in Texas.

The sun was really shining on me, birds were singing, music was playing—to hell with the *Banner-Democrat*, the Chamber of Commerce, the chief, and the rest of the griping SOBs.

The next day, just by using the telephone directory service, I found—guess what?—not Geoffrey but George, the old man. When

Geoffrey got out of the psychiatric, he went to his dad.

I got onto the sheriff in Shivers County right away, explained that he had two murder suspects on his territory, and asked him to check on their whereabouts in the neighborhood of June 6. In the meantime, I felt it was worth it to continue investigating those Garden Club women.

Nina's Notes

Notices by Nina Norton

Wedding bells have been ringing in the ears of Mr. and Mrs. Ted Osterman, and they are going to follow their sound north to Philadelphia, Pennsylvania for the rites which on next Thursday will join their grandson Kirk to Miss Evelyn Dungannon of that city. Bravo Kirk! And bravo Ted and Ginnie for the fine grandson! And bravo to Ethyl and Albert Osterman, parents of the groom.

XVI

Sound the Alarm

HARRIET BUSHROW

The minute I read "Nina's Notes" on July 3, I called Lieutenant Cochran on the phone.

"Lieutenant," I said, "if you are as clever as I think you are, you can catch the burglar that has caused you such grief."

"How?"

"Well," I said," if you read 'Nina's Notes' in the paper this morning, you'd know how. Your crime wave is going to strike again and it is going to be at 1710 West Avenue."

"Say that again; I don't think I heard it right."

"Oh, you heard it right enough. Nina simply notifies your burglar and the whole illegal part of our society that Virginia Osterman and Ted will be away from home on that day and the day before and no doubt on the day after."

"I see what you mean."

"If you just will, you can make a mousetrap of this little jaunt the Ostermans are taking. In February—or maybe it was March—there was a story about Virginia, that's Mrs. Osterman, and her silver tea caddies. She collects them, you see."

I waited for the lieutenant to say something, but he didn't.

"Don't you see?"

"Mrs. Bushrow," he said, "I appreciate your interest, but this kind of robbery has never occurred in that part of town. The police can't put a man on duty to watch every house just because someone is going out of town."

Just like that! I had it in mind to say, "You'll be sorry." But you don't catch flies with vinegar.

"Of course you can't," I said, "but this is not 'every house'—this is the house of a collector who has some very valuable tea caddies, things that are too large to keep in a safe deposit box—things that were practically advertised in that article in the *Banner-Democrat*, a large picture of Virginia with three or four of those lovely things right in front of her on the table.

"And here 'Nina's Notes' says she and Ted are going to be away, even gives the best time to break in—Thursday night, when they are at the wedding in Philadelphia."

"I'll have the patrol car check the house every hour," he said.

Psh, that didn't amount to anything. A burglar clever enough to read "Nina's Notes" and other notices and figure out the best time and just where to break in—well, somebody like that knows the patrol cars just sneak along in residential areas, not going anywhere in particular and therefore in no hurry. Other cars that are out at two-thirty in the morning are either going home and to bed or else to the emergency room at the hospital or something like that.

All our thief has to do is crouch down in the shadows somewhere and wait for the patrol car to dawdle by—going twenty miles an hour, most likely. Then, when the patrol car passes and maybe throws a light on the front of the house, the burglar hiding in the bushes knows it will be an hour before the police sail by again.

Patrol car, indeed! All the same, I gave Lieutenant Cochran his chance.

And sure enough! Here's a clipping from the July 11 *Banner-Democrat:*

Collection Decimated in Robbery

Mrs. T. F. Osterman returned from the wedding of her grandson in Philadelphia to find that her home at 1710 West Avenue had been entered and nine silver tea caddies dating from the 1700s stolen. The items stolen were the cream of a collection formed over a lifetime.

According to Mrs. Osterman, the value of the items stolen is estimated at about $50,000. "Of course," she stated, "that's at auction. Melted down, the silver would bring very much less.

"Fortunately," Mrs. Osterman observed, "the thief did not touch my porcelain caddies, some of which are far more valuable than the silver examples that were taken."

I carefully refrained from calling the good lieutenant to say, "I told you so," which is about the most aggravating thing you can say to anybody.

Of course, I didn't have to say a thing about the robbery to poor Lieutenant Cochran. The next day's editorial in the *Banner-Democrat* said it all. I have the clipping, all right;

but I'm not going to insert it here because it doesn't say anything new. Public outrage is pretty generally all the same. After you've said, "Ain't it awful?" all you can do is say it again.

But the newspaper people make a living by writing such things, and the people who buy the papers like to see somebody agree with them in print.

Then, two days later, in the readers' column, there was a letter from Reverend Arthur Everdy, and I am going to include it, because what he said is true—and then you'll see what happened afterward. Here it is:

To the *Borderville Banner-Democrat:*
A great outcry has arisen in response to the absolute siege of robberies which the good people of Southwest Virginia and Upper East Tennessee have been obliged to endure. Readers will remember the robberies at the Larken, Peterson, and Duffy residences in Burke County; at the Harmon, Douglas, Barnwell, Simmons, and Epperson homes in Ambrose County; and at the Sudberry, Dangerfield, Brinker, and Hedgecox residences in Borderville, Virginia, while there have been incidents at the Donaldson, Vernon, Claymore, and Frothmore homes in Borderville, Tennessee. The robbery at the Osterman residence on July 10 brings the number of robberies in our region to sixteen in the past six months.

"What," we may ask, "has brought this wave of crime to our area?" We ask it to no avail. The only answer that can be made is

116

that social conditions have so deteriorated in this beloved country of ours that the lives of our young people have lost direction. It becomes incumbent, therefore, on responsible citizens to support those organizations seeking to develop character and ideals in our youth both for their good and the safety of the rest of us.

I wish to recommend the Hand of Fellowship, an organization for which I have the privilege to be a board member in Borderville. This work, which has been operating here a little over a year, has a membership of 57 disadvantaged youths. It is their goal through wholesome social and athletic activities to keep these young gentlemen on the road to a satisfying and productive life.

I strongly urge the support of this organization.

Rev. Arthur Everdy

XVII

The July Meeting

LEOTA KELSEY

I guess I need to tell you about the next meeting. I had been looking forward to this one because it would be at Camille Hythorp's place and I wanted to see what she had done to it. Other things, however, would become more interesting.

The Buena Vista Garden Club never had such a summer as this last one. You would think that after Rita had been gone a month or so, things would settle down. But that was not to be.

Don Cochran had somehow gotten it in his head that it was somebody in the club who hit Rita with the squirrel and left her to suffocate in that pile of peat moss. None of our members ever said it couldn't be so. I imagine any one of us might have a good enough reason to be angry with her, but when it came to putting the finger on one of us who could have done a thing like that, we couldn't believe it.

But that Don Cochran! He seemed to have this idea that it was a woman who killed Rita. And when you think about it, you have to agree that he might be right.

The person—man or woman—who did it, committed the murder, hadn't intended to kill Rita when he or she went over there to Rita's place. He—and I think it would have been a man if it was planned ahead of time—would have had a gun or knife if he had intended murder all along. But it would be more like a woman to flare up and hit Rita with the nearest thing handy, especially if while they were arguing and all het up, Rita coolly turned her back as if to say, "You can go to the devil for all I care."

And so, it really could be any of us. Rita had such a way of stepping on other people's bunions. We put up with it because she was a McDurrie and her grandmother organized the club, and because she was rich, and because she could get things done when nobody else could. But someone will let a person like Rita walk over them just so long before it all comes out. And if there is a concrete squirrel handy, who knows what someone might do with it?

Still, a sudden flare-up like that doesn't mean someone actually wanted to kill Rita. We just couldn't believe that any member of the Buena Vista Club would leave a person to smother in peat moss.

But there was Don Cochran, and it began to look like he was going down the list of Buena Vista members. You already know about Viola Coleport and Pauline Giesley.

Don had them on the carpet asking every kind of question and still couldn't find any evidence, but he didn't actually clear one suspect before he went to the next, which was the worst part of it. Imagine what it would be like to be badgered by the city detective and feeling that he might come back at you again and again. Of course, you would know you were innocent, but I can't think it would be fun.

Well, the latest of Don Cochran's suspects was Laura Gooding.

Laura is a sweet little thing. She is in the club because her mother-in-law was an important member; she's been dead now for fifteen years or more. Laura is like me. Her folks didn't have money and weren't big shots. She really wasn't what you would expect to find in a club like the Buena Vista. I suppose old Mrs. Gooding proposed her daughter-in-law for membership in an effort to build Laura up.

I was not a member of the club at the time, but I have heard that Laura offended Rita once—a little thing that nobody else would take the least notice of.

It seems the club was searching for a beautification project. The old McDurrie Coffin Works, being no longer used by the Gaulton Furniture Company, was standing vacant down by the tracks just off Stonewall Drive. It was in bad shape, with windows all knocked out and holes in the roof. In fact, it caught fire when some bums were living in it later. So it really looked pretty bad when the Buena Vista was looking for a way to "make Borderville beautiful."

Poor Laura! She apparently thought she had a really good idea when she suggested that the club could perhaps get the city to tear down "that old eyesore."

Too bad for Laura that "that old eyesore" just happened to be the source of the McDurrie wealth, and although the old works had been out of the family for all those years and years,

Rita took offense. After all, it was *her* grandfather who built the hideous old thing, and Rita wasn't going to let it be called an eyesore.

Old Mrs. Gooding made Laura apologize to Rita, which apparently was the wrong thing to do, because Laura made it worse instead of better. And though Rita had to accept the apology, she was always very cool to Laura from that time on.

All of this came to a head last fall when Laura's daughter, Margo, went off to Giles College, which is the same college where Rita went. I don't know too much about how those things are handled because I didn't go to college. Bob and I got married during the Korean War and more school just didn't seem to be the thing I needed. It never bothered me; I'm perfectly happy with my life the way it is. But it really bothers some people that they missed out on college. And one of these people is Laura Gooding.

It doesn't amount to a whip stitch to me that someone has read all that poetry and knows all about art. They can't possibly be any happier than I am. But Laura—she's always trying to make up for something, and she lays quite a load on Margo. The child had to do absolutely everything other girls—those from the "silk-stocking" families—were doing: ballet, horseback riding, whatever was being done. It was like Laura poured everything into that girl.

So, one of the things poor Margo had to do was join the best sorority at Giles.

I don't know a thing in this world about such things, but I understand a girl is "rushed," and then the sorority decides just which girls they want to take in.

Now you can rest assured that when Rita Claymore went to college, she knew how to get into the very best sorority on campus. And you can bet your boots she never let the sorority forget who she was. So when it came time for the sorority to choose their new members, Margo didn't get in.

That was hard on the girl, but it was worse on the mother. Laura had it in her head that Rita was the one that kept Margo out.

Hell hath no fury like a woman that thinketh her one lone chick has been wronged. This was doubly true in Laura's case because she remembered all those slights from Rita she had had to endure over the years.

Who knows how Don Cochran got hold of the way the two women felt about each other? But apparently he knew about it, because he lit in to Laura, gave her a taste of the third degree, and scared the poor woman nearly to death.

Maybe you think the telephone wires weren't hot as soon as word got out about Laura and her troubles with Don Cochran. A thing like that is not an item for just anybody in a town the size of ours, but for members of Buena Vista it was a way of life for the next two days.

The suggestion of a member of the club doing such a terrible thing to Rita did not rest easy with me. We think we have gone beyond such things, but someone had taken the first small step to commit a big crime. It was comforting to find others who felt the same way.

We looked at the matter every way it could be looked at. When one of us would think of another angle, that would set us off on another round of calls. I bet I was on the phone for five or six hours those first two days, and I would have been on the line longer if I hadn't needed to go to the stove.

There were those of our members, you see, that had a perfect right to be angry with Rita. The first one was Pauline Giesley, who was mad at Rita, first, because she had embarrassed her by bringing charges against her that she cheated at the flower show. And in the second place, Rita attacked Pauline's character. In the third place, Rita prevented Pauline from taking one of the prizes, because Pauline is just very good at arranging.

The second member who had a right to be angry with Rita was her own sister, Viola, who needed money—not for herself, mind, but, as some of the ladies knew and the rest soon learned, for her nephew, Rita's stepson. And Rita wouldn't give it to her. I don't think for a minute that Viola would have minded being turned down if the money had been for her; but it was for Rita's own stepson, who needed it badly, and that makes a big difference.

And then this business about the sorority popped up. Now, I do admit that I don't have quite the sympathy for Laura that I do for the other two. Yes, Laura was upset when her daughter was not asked to join the sorority her mother thought was best. I'm sure that Margo Gooding herself was disappointed, but Laura's disappointment was for herself. She wanted to be able to say, "My daughter is in this fine sorority." So there's a kind of double strength to her anger there.

Then somebody pointed out that our club had been struck twice by thieves—the one that got away with all of Rita's silver, and the one that stole Enid Frothmore's jewelry. Anyone would have to admit that one murder, two robberies, and three members suspected by police is enough to whip any organization into a conversational frenzy.

This chatter about our club's problem was not at all bad for the attendance at our July meeting. Camille's living room opens out onto a patio next to a large swimming pool. She opened the sliding glass doors so that our meeting was almost like being outdoors. From where I was sitting, I could easily see the bronze sculpture Camille got on her last trip to the Indian reservation out in New Mexico. Its solemn warrior serves as the centerpiece of a rock garden practically growing out of the flagstones around the pool.

Although the chairs and sofas in that room have the plushest upholstery, no one was going to fall asleep that day. Of course, we buzzed quite a bit about what was on everybody's mind. When we looked around, we saw that Enid Frothmore was present, but neither Viola Coleport nor Laura Gooding was there.

124

Dodo Peterson said, "Well, if we are going to drop out of the Buena Vista one by one every time Don Cochran gets suspicious, we'll be in bad shape pretty soon."

Dodo has a strong voice, and several of the ladies heard what she said and joined in.

"There's got to be an end to it sometime," Judith Belford said.

Someone said, yes, that was true, but that didn't do us much good in the meantime.

Then I said—I don't put myself forward too much, but this time I said—"Bob thinks we ought to get Mrs. Bushrow to solve the mystery for us." Of course I knew those two had actually been rummaging around in Rita's yard.

I don't know why, but just at that instant, everyone in the room stopped talking and I was surprised to hear my voice come out so strong. I looked around and was really embarrassed.

"Harriet Bushrow!" Gladys Weaver said. "Isn't she beyond anything like that now?"

Mrs. Bushrow is ninety-six years old, but my Bob swears by her. And when you think about it, she got to the bottom of the Historical Society mystery last year in spite of a broken hip. I pointed this out.

"Do you suppose she would do it for us?" Dodo inquired.

"It wouldn't hurt to ask," Judith pointed out.

Then Dodo said, "Let's put it before the club when the meeting begins."

So that was what we did, and the motion passed.

After the meeting, we all went into the dining room for refreshments. Camille can only do things in a big way—especially the little things—and she had outdone herself with three cakes, coffee, tea, *and* punch, and numerous large platters of munchies. I commented that the massive Empire sideboard reminded me of one an aunt had had back in my childhood.

"Oh, I got that in a furniture store in Roanoke," Camille responded. "It's actually brand-new—made in North Carolina."

I thought how like Harriet Bushrow that was: the grandeur of a former time on the outside and up to the minute with everything on the inside. If anyone could help the club, it would be her. She would even appreciate that a member had her style of furniture—even if it was a reproduction.

I called Harriet that evening and gave her the official commission.

XVIII

Pennies from Heaven

HARRIET BUSHROW

It was July 22. I'm glad to say that they didn't put it in the paper.

Mary Lizabeth and I had our supper; and after the dear child washed the dishes, we watched *Murder, She Wrote* on TV.

I have always liked Angela Lansbury. I remember when she first began playing parts in movies. She had such a sweet face, and she is still just as pretty as ever.

Of course, she's better at solving things than I am. She nabs the culprit in just one hour. All she has to do is find one little slip-up that the killer has made and put it to him. And then everything is all cleared up. The one who did it—whatever it was—owns up to everything.

But when I work on a crime, it seems like it takes forever.

Well, as I say, on July 22 we had our supper and watched television. Then we played three games of dominoes. I beat Mary Lizabeth one game, and she beat me two. She is good at dominoes.

After that it thundered just a little, and I told Mary Lizabeth to shut all the windows.

Now, my house is old—not as old as I am, but it's old. And if you've lived in an old house, you know that after a certain time the sash cords begin to go. If the cord on one side only goes, that's not so bad, because you can still open the window if you hold your mouth just so, and it will stay open. But if the cords on both sides go, you have to get a stick to prop the sash up if you want the window open.

Anybody who doesn't know about the window with no sash cords might open it in such a way that the sash would stay up for just a little while because it got jimmied sideways a little bit and was jammed in the window frame. But after a while, the wind—or maybe it is the vibration of a big truck going by—will shake the sash free and it will come down with a bang.

What I'm getting at is that the kitchen window that looks out onto my backyard hasn't got the sign of a sash cord and hasn't had for twenty years more or less. So, when Mary Lizabeth closed that window, she took away the stick I use to hold the sash up.

Well, the storm didn't last very long, but that was the reason why the window was shut and the stick wasn't in it.

Mary Lizabeth has to be at the Cup and Saucer by seven, so we don't stay up very late.

There we were, sleeping the sleep of the just, when suddenly I woke up. I didn't know just what the noise that woke me up was, but I got the impression of glass falling, which is just what it was. That window sash in the kitchen had come down with a crash, breaking the glass, you see, and I suppose a fragment of it didn't fall right away, but sort of slid out of the groove and broke up when it hit the floor.

"What's that!" I said, as soon as I got my eyes open.

I didn't get an answer, but I could see this shape just there at the door of my bedroom.

"Stop where you are!"

Whoever it was kept coming—silent as the night itself.

"I say, stop!"

At that I reached over to turn on the light that's on the stand beside my bed.

Most of my possessions are not very valuable, but my furniture is a different matter. I pride myself on my furniture. When I was first married, many of our friends were buying what was popular then—made in Grand Rapids, most of it. Overstuffed chairs! I thought those things were horrible then, and time has proved me right.

Yes, indeed.

Well, I don't know why I did such a smart thing; but you see, Lamar and I started out with just a few things that our families let us have. And as luck would have it, they were beautiful mahogany things that were so out of date that nobody wanted them. Then, as time went on, I picked up other pieces to go with what I had— got them at junky second-hand prices. And now I've got a fortune in antebellum furniture.

So, I have this sewing cabinet—a lovely little thing on a pedestal with splayed legs; and I use it for a nightstand beside my bed. I keep a lamp there and my Bible and a box of Kleenex; and last thing before I go to bed, I put my glasses there. And something else I have there—Lamar's old service revolver.

Well, with this thing coming toward me, I reached for that pistol. But in doing so, I knocked over my sewing cabinet; and it went down with everything on it, including the revolver, right on the floor.

What with the lamp breaking and that heavy revolver skittering across the bare floor, there was quite a racket.

The fellow hesitated. Even a burglar gets puzzled once in a while.

Lord have mercy, I thought. What do I do now?

I guess the Lord heard me, because the next thing I saw was this white figure coming through the door—an avenging angel if there ever was one.

It turned to the left and picked up something from the top of the beautiful crotch mahogany chest that I have there, and I knew immediately what it was.

My "angel" raised that thing up and brought it down with all her strength on the poor fellow's head. It was the antique Dresden cachepot that I keep my pennies in. Of course it broke and the pennies scattered everywhere.

The fellow said, "Damn!" dropped his flashlight, and put his hands to his head.

Then he said, "Hell!"

I yelled, "Call nine-one-one! Call nine-one-one!" and the angelic Mary Lizabeth disappeared into the hall to do it.

Then our intruder said something that I'm not going to repeat and staggered out of the room.

Quick as I could get my old bones out of the bed, I followed and got to the hall, where Mary Lizabeth had put the light on. I got a glimpse of our burglar as he raced into the kitchen.

He had on black trousers, black windbreaker, black ski mask, which was why he wasn't knocked completely out when Mary Lizabeth hit him with my cachepot.

"You told them we had a burglary?"

She said, "Yes."

"And gave them the address?"

"Yes."

Well, of course she gave them the address. Mary Lizabeth is no dumb bunny. Just because she was my literacy student and couldn't read until I taught her doesn't make her stupid. Look at how clever she was to hit that fellow with my cachepot.

We went to the kitchen, and sure enough, there was the glass all over the floor. Our burglar had gone out by the same window he had come in by—through the sash, this time, instead of under it. There were jagged pieces of glass still clinging in the grooves in the wood. If the man hadn't had on gloves and that windbreaker, he would have cut himself for sure and maybe we would have had DNA for evidence. But in real-life detection, you can't expect too much good luck.

About that time we heard the police car. I grabbed my robe right quickly before I went to the door.

The officer looked at everything—went in the backyard. He said the man must have

131

gone out the alley, which anybody ought to know anyhow. He showed us how the burglar had made a hole in the screen and pried the hook loose. Then he had just taken the screen off, quietly set it on the ground, and left it leaning against my rhododendron bush.

Then the officer got after us for not locking our sash at the top. Well, now, that's a fine thing when folks without air conditioning have to lock their windows shut in the month of July.

All in all, he made it sound like it was our fault the man had gotten in the house. I just thought, Wait till I tell Don Cochran about you. But of course I didn't get around to talking to Don Cochran until later.

The fact is, I was rather glad to see the young man go; he even gave me a lecture on being careful with revolvers!

We left everything just the way it was and went to bed. In the morning I mourned over my broken cachepot and the lamp that had gotten broken. It was an old one—electrified—it was one that Mother had had. But my sewing cabinet was as good as ever and my glasses were all right.

After a while I returned to my right mind and said, "Well, you old ninny, why are you cut up over a lamp and a cachepot that got broken? Don't you know you are going to die in a year or two and leave all these things behind? You just better be glad you didn't make that last journey last night."

When I put it that way, I was pretty well satisfied with things as they were, because this old girl is not ready to kick off just yet.

That sweet Mary Lizabeth had picked up all those pennies off the floor before she left for work. Just for the fun of it, I started to count them. After I got to fifteen hundred, I quit. That's fifteen dollars, and there were a lot more pennies besides.

It's little wonder the poor fellow was wobbly when he left the house.

Pennies from heaven! My goodness! Think of the earthly places our blessings come from.

XIX

The Command Post Is Set Up

BOB KELSEY

"There was an intruder in Harriet Bushrow's house, and she was attacked."

Leota offered this information as she hung up the telephone.

"That was Beverly Henley, who lives across the street from Harriet. It seems she's all right, but I wonder how many of her nine lives she has left."

I must say this is not the first time Harriet Bushrow has faced dangerous criminals and lived to tell the tale. In fact, there was one time when I was supposed to be protecting her as she confronted a murderer, but I turned out to be no help at all and was the one who went to the hospital. Although I could not have prevented the current incident, I felt that I really should go see Mrs. Bushrow.

I took the van over to her place and knocked on the door. Mary Lizabeth had gone off to her job, so Mrs. Bushrow came to the door.

"We have been having a bit of excitement here," she said. "Won't you come in and see what our crime wave has washed up?"

Between sympathetic comments on my part, she showed me the burglar's damage and recounted the whole scene. She had just been counting pennies when I came in. I agree that Mary Lizabeth is heaven-sent, but

Harriet Bushrow has been given her own special graces.

After our tour, Mrs. Bushrow and I sat down in her sitting room.

"This was a total surprise. I did not see this coming," she said.

I pointed out that most burglaries are that way.

"Oh, I knew that the Ostermans were going to be robbed." She proceeded to explain how the information in "Nina's Notes" could be used to plan a burglary. Taking an envelope of clippings from her desk, she laid out the social columns and the corresponding robbery reports.

"Of course the paper didn't announce *my* intruder. They must think I deserve special treatment."

"Well, do you think it is the same person responsible for the other burglaries?" I asked. "It could be a freelancer."

"Yes, it's the same outfit." Mrs. Bushrow said this with a twinkle in her eyes. "And they don't rely on just the paper to figure out their plans."

She proceeded to tell me of her encounter with the Reverend Alec Boheem and how he was interested in her gold-headed cane.

"And there is more to it than just that," she went on. "Do you remember that pin we found at Rita's place?"

"Yes," I answered as she brought out her drawing of the trinket.

"Well, Alec Boheem has a group called

ICD. Now, look at this pin. It's an 'I' and a 'C' and a 'D' all jammed together."

"There seems to be another 'I' attached to the end."

"I haven't quite figured that out. It could mean something more, or it could be there to make it symmetrical.

"Anyhow, I want to find out more about that bunch," she continued. "It is some kind of secret order."

I pointed out that we needed a surveillance effort.

"Yes, but a surveillance from within, and I know who can help us out: Slater Watts."

"But will he be willing to do it after all he has been through?"

"I think Lily Dabney would be able to persuade him to help out; besides, where else are we going to get an honest juvenile delinquent?"

I agreed with this, and we discussed how it could be managed.

XX

Surprises

DON COCHRAN

Life is full of surprises. You think you've seen it all, and then something new comes up.

Sergeant Banks came into my office on that morning and said, "Did you hear that Mrs. Bushrow had a break-in last night? It's sort of ironic, isn't it, since she saw the Osterman incident coming?"

"I am sure the burglar met his match. The world would have many fewer robbers around if they all knew the Mrs. Bushrows who live among us."

It was a bit gratifying that the criminals were having their own troubles.

That afternoon I got a phone call. "Lieutenant Cochran, this is Mrs. L. Q. C. Lamar Bushrow. May I pay you a call this afternoon? How about in a few minutes?"

By this time I had read the report and knew not only that this woman had just had an intruder invade her residence and try to attack her, but that she and her housemate had actually had the excitement of repulsing him. Add to this that she is over ninety. Undoubtedly, she wants to talk to me about all this, and she makes it sound like a social occasion. How could I refuse? In addition to being on the front page and the editorial page, I guess I'll end up in "Nina's Notes."

"Of course you can, Mrs. Bushrow."

"Good. Bob Kelsey and Slater Watts will be coming with me."

It sounded like I would have to go through a receiving line!

In about half an hour, here they all came and took up the chairs in my office.

"Here is Bob Kelsey," Mrs. Bushrow said, "and I think you remember Slater Watts."

Of course I nodded. Now if I had forgotten, John Cinic at the *Banner-Democrat* would remind me. The kid seemed a bit uncomfortable, and I don't blame him.

Mrs. Bushrow settled in and began: "Do you recollect that pin that Bob Kelsey and I found over at Rita's?"

"Yes."

"Well, I think my intruder may have indicated what it all means. As you know, most of our burglaries—at least the ones in recent months—get 'announced' in 'Nina's Notes.' Now, there was nothing in the paper to alert someone about my little house being worth any attention or being left unattended last night. That's because I am an old homebody, and my place has very little that a criminal could use. My robber came anyway. So he must have selected me another way."

She then proceeded to tell me about her encounter with the Reverend Alec Boheem and how he had been very interested in her gold-tipped cane.

"Mrs. Bushrow," I said, "covetousness may be prohibited by the Ten Commandments, but it does not necessarily lead to stealing."

Mrs. Bushrow's eyes brightened.

"The Reverend Boheem runs an organization which I understood at first to be called the Circle of Isedee but turns out to be the Circle of ICD," she said. "If you look at the pin we found—the one from Rita's place—you will see that it is an 'I,' a 'C,' and a 'D' all squeezed together."

I had already pulled the Claymore file and had it on my desk. I took the pin from inside and examined it through its plastic bag.

"Ah, but what about the extra 'I' on the end?"

"That hasn't been figured out yet, but if we knew the whole story, where would the suspense be?"

Bob Kelsey now started talking.

"This suggests a link from ICD to Rita's murder and the robbery at her house. The question is, how do we prove the connection?"

"I certainly couldn't go on just this," I said. "No court of law would render a conviction with a pin that *might* spell out the initials of an organization.

"I have several women with delicious motives to go after Marguerite Claymore. One of them even had an argument over money with her at three P.M. the day before she left for Knoxville. In addition there is a nest of family members in Texas who will be benefiting from all this. But even when I have had more evidence, the court of the *Banner-Democrat* has not been enthusiastic. Again, Slater, I apologize for arresting you."

Slater Watts acknowledged the last statement with a nod.

"If this group is involved, they will show up at another robbery," I summed up.

"Obviously," Bob Kelsey said, "you could set up an ambush the next time Nina notifies the burglars that a house will be left alone. However, the Reverend Boheem could dismiss the kid you catch by declaring that he had just 'relapsed.' Besides, you would only have solved one robbery and maybe prevented several; we would still have a murderer to find."

"We might be able to get the lout we caught to talk."

"From all I have heard, this organization is run like a gang. Gangs foster great loyalty.

"We will get further if someone infiltrates the group and finds the information that is needed," Kelsey said. "This is where you come in, Lieutenant Cochran. Slater Watts here has agreed to be our spy. What we need from you is a recommendation to the Reverend Boheem that his group would be good for Slater. You could say that one of the reasons you arrested Slater was because he had a criminal record and was suspected of doing other things."

"Oh no you don't! I've done enough to foul up Slater's life already, without suggesting that he has some phantom criminal past. I am going to lie low for a while and save up my chits for when I need to do something really unpopular."

Mrs. Bushrow drew herself up. Her hand was on her gold-headed cane. It was more like a scepter.

"Lieutenant Cochran," she said in her

most gracious southern voice, "we need a person of authority who knows Slater's record to contact Reverend Boheem. Now, Slater's parents could bring him to ICD, but gangs—from what I hear—thrive on boys from broken homes. Boheem will be more receptive if the parents are not involved."

I could see myself headed for trouble. Maybe Slater would take me off the hook.

"Slater, are you willing to go through with this?"

"Yes, sir. Mrs. Claymore was my boss. I feel like I should help find her murderer."

What a fine kid. And this was after I had put him in jail on suspicion of that very same crime.

"Now, Slater, Mrs. Bushrow talked about how a gang can swallow you up if your family is not strong. Do your parents approve of this scheme?"

"Yes, sir."

A direct, respectful answer, without any wavering. The boy would have been good in the military.

Slater was not going to back down: I was probably going to have to go along, but I then got a revelation.

"Mr. Kelsey, why couldn't that associate pastor at the church—Debbie Mollusk—why couldn't she be the one to contact Reverend Boheem?"

"I hadn't thought of that."

"Why, Lieutenant Cochran, that is so clever of you," chimed in Mrs. Bushrow.

I tell you, I beamed. The sky was sunny again.

Bob Kelsey paused for a moment and said,

"That would work. Could I tell her that the police suspect Slater of other misbehavior?"

"Just say that he has given us a lot of trouble; but whatever you do, don't use my name."

Bob Kelsey said that would work.

I turned to Slater and said, "I wish you lots of luck. And by the way, if you are going to be a juvenile delinquent, you're going to have to stop calling people 'sir.' "

Slater broke out in a big smile.

Everyone shuffled out of the office.

We had a good lead, and we were zeroing in on the target. I had actually been able to make a successful suggestion to Mrs. L. Q. C. Lamar Bushrow. What a surprise.

XXI

Mission Begun

SLATER WATTS

Mr. Kelsey and Mrs. Bushrow got me into this. They came over one day this summer. Mrs. Bushrow had been robbed the night before. My parents thought that was awful. I thought it was awful. You see, Mrs. Bushrow got me out of jail!

Anyhow, Mr. Kelsey and Mrs. Bushrow came to see me. Mrs. Bushrow told me that Reverend Alec Boheem's group, ICD, had done her robbery. She wanted someone to join the group to see what it does. Since I had a "past" as a juvenile delinquent, she asked me to be her spy. I said yes.

Then we all went and saw Detective Cochran down at the police station. He is a much nicer man when he is not arresting you. He suggested that we have the lady preacher at Mr. Kelsey's church recommend me, and so we did.

Mr. Kelsey became my contact, because his house is on the way home. He told me to write a journal.

This is the first top-secret report from Slater Watts, Private Eye.

ICD is the local branch of the Hand of Fellowship, and it meets in the dining hall of the True Path Church. There is a meeting every Tuesday and Thursday afternoon, and we have to go to church on Sunday. Reverend

Boheem welcomed me warmly. "It is so won-derful to have a true son of Egypt among us!" he said. I don't know about that.

Reverend Boheem has an assistant named Jon Sidan. He told me I had to sit at the low end of the inner circle. The other "brothers" came in and filled in the two circles. Then Rev-erend Boheem walked to the center of the cir-cles. There is something about him that attracts your attention.

"Brothers, we have a new friend to join our fraternity. Slater Watts has fallen in the world's eyes, but we will lift him up. We will give him strength to triumph over the world. Slater, do you want to rise?"

"Yes, Reverend Boheem."

"Do you want to feel good?"

"Yes."

"Do you want to feel the power?"

"Yes."

"Come here to the middle, and brothers, let us place the Hand of Fellowship upon Slater."

I moved to the center of the circle, and the "brothers" laid their hands on my shoulders and head. Those who could not reach me put their hands on the arms of the closer guys. There were about forty of them all reaching for me.

"Tell him what you think of him."

"We love you, Slater!"

"Tell him what he can do."

"You can reach the top!"

We all returned to our seats.

"Josh Stahl, stand forth and give the oath and duties of the First Order."

At this point, a guy with shoulder-length

hair got up. Jon Sidan gave him a sheet of paper to read.

"Slater Watts," he said, "the Hand of Fellowship is a community of orders. For each order, you must swear an oath. To enter the First Order, you must give your loyalty to your brothers and commit to never divulging the activities of the group nor revealing the secrets of a higher order to a lower. Are you ready to join our brotherhood?"

I said, "Yes."

"Raise your left hand, and place your right hand on the Book of Fellowship."

Jon Sidan brought out a fancy book with a lock on it. I repeated the oath line by line. It was all about supporting the brothers and recognizing Reverend Boheem as my master and not telling a soul about any of it. Of course, I would have to tell everything to Mr. Kelsey, but I figured it was "supporting the brothers" if I told the truth about them. But, man, I didn't like breaking a promise.

Reverend Boheem looked at me. He has eyes that go through you.

"Slater Watts, you are now a man of the First Order in the Isis Command Division of the Hand of Fellowship. Again, let me stress the secrecy of what I am going to say to you. Our local fraternity is named after the Egyptian goddess Isis, but you must never reveal her name to anyone. You may only refer to our division by its initials, ICD.

"The Hand of Fellowship has nine orders. In order for you to progress to the Second

Order, you will need to complete a task that I will assign you."

Jon Sidan strummed the guitar, we sang three songs, and my initiation was over—and I was glad it was over. Actually, it was better than I thought it would be.

Next, we played basketball out on the court. David Gregory, Jerry Glasgow, Josh Stahl, and Rob Davis were on my team.

During a break, Josh Stahl came over to me and said, "Are you worried about rising in ICD, kid?"

"A little bit."

"Don't worry. It'll be a piece of cake. I got to Third Order in no time."

We all got to eat supper. Some of the guys had been in the kitchen cooking. It was just hot dogs and beans, but I will take a free meal anytime.

After supper, I found out what my task is to get to Second Order. I am supposed to clean up the dining hall for four meetings. I suppose that isn't too bad. I got right to work. Most of the guys went to other parts of the building. Higher orders have other "projects" to work on.

Jon Sidan was working down the hall in the office as I started mopping the floors. Suddenly, I heard him cry out, "Damn, I've lost the file."

Well, that wasn't the kind of language I was used to hearing at a church.

I heard Reverend Boheem talking to Jon Sidan in a raised voice. I laid down the mop and walked down to the office. I just had to see what was going on.

Reverend Boheem was saying, "Jon, that file had an important part of our database. I hope you made a backup?"

"I did, but it was last month. I'll have to retype all the new data back into the computer."

"Well, that'll make you learn your lesson."

"Excuse me, Reverend Boheem," I said, "but have you tried to use undelete?"

No, they didn't know about that. So I sat down at the keyboard. They didn't have the Windows version on their system, but I was able to use the DOS one. Shazam! The file was recovered.

"Slater, that's marvelous," said Reverend Boheem. "I'm going to switch you over to working on the computer. Jon, what needs to be done?"

"There are a lot of contributions that need to be entered."

"Slater, you can do those instead of cleaning the dining hall, and also make backup copies of each of the databases. Regularly."

That was my first day with the Hand of Fellowship.

Say, this writing bit isn't so bad. In school we were always getting those essays where we were supposed to write about "the best summer I ever had" or "the worst birthday in my family" or something else I had mostly forgotten. Sometimes we would have to make a list of adjectives and then use as many as we could in a paragraph. It made me hate adjectives. This ICD stuff is real and happening now. I can just let the words flow.

XXII

Talking to the Plants

BOB KELSEY

I had arranged for Slater Watts to come over on Monday, Wednesday, and Friday mornings. Ostensibly, he was going to help me out with the garden.

He had been working for Charlotte Wisp at that time, but she was uncomfortable with having someone who had been in jail around her house. I don't think Charlotte has a mean bone in her body: she just hasn't thought through that being in jail and being convicted are two different things. We all have our foibles, but we would be much better off if we all took some time and exercised our brains a little more.

Slater was handling all this well. Harriet Bushrow had explained to him that as his name was already tied to Rita's death, he might as well take the role of hero. He seemed to have taken to the part quite easily.

Slater appeared at our house in jeans and a T-shirt. I ushered him into the backyard.

"I went to ICD last night," he said.

"Well, what happened?"

"I can't rightly tell you because I swore that I wouldn't tell a soul outside the group."

I was beginning not to like this outfit already. They had something to hide.

"You swore not to tell a soul?"

"Yes."

"I must say, Slater, I admire your commitment to honor."

I had not really looked at the situation in this light. Was it honorable to break an oath to fight the bad guys?

Slater grinned at this point. "Mr. Kelsey, you still need some work around here. I could tell your gladiolas all about last night. They don't have souls. I know you'll be out of earshot."

"Actually, I feel sleepy. I think I'll pull this lawn chair over just behind you and fall asleep under the newspaper."

Slater was enjoying how I played along with his game. He got down on his knees and started telling the gladiolas about the Isis Command Division—the story you heard in the previous chapter.

I was relieved that he had not been made to do much more than sweep the floor. With all the secrecy, I had sort of wondered if they would make him do something illegal.

When he got to the end, I "awoke" from my nap and said, "Slater, why don't we take a break?"

"I didn't know you were back there, Mr. Kelsey," he said slyly.

We both laughed.

Now, to keep up this charade, I had to pretend that I had not heard the story. I got two soft drinks out of the refrigerator, and we sat down in the kitchen.

"You know, Slater, I bet you are going to have a lot of information about this ICD bunch. You are going to have a lot in your journal. You could probably put it on the computer, but I bet it would be hard to keep it away from someone else who also used the same machine, wouldn't it?"

"Yeah."

"In fact, I bet someone like you would be able to find the information somehow."

"They probably could."

"This someone could take your words and put them on one of those disk things?"

"That would be the easy part."

We mulled over some other topics; then Slater returned to the garden. Later on, I paid him for his efforts and watched him ride off on his bicycle.

I would wait two days for his next report.

XXIII

I Have a Talk with Viola Coleport

HARRIET BUSHROW

Wasn't that sweet of Leota Kelsey to have the Buena Vista Garden Club make me "their" detective? One of the things she said was, "Now you can probably get something out of Viola Coleport."

Of course I've been working on this thing all along. I have found that a little old lady can do *anything* she pleases—so long as her bones are still holding her up. Usually it requires a bit of thinking and a bit of patience. But I can use fewer schemes to find things out if I have an "official" capacity.

I asked Leota if the club was going to give me a badge, and what do you know, the next time I saw Bob Kelsey, he had made one for me. He had done it on a piece of typing paper. It looks like the patches Don Cochran wears on his uniform, except it says: "Buena Vista Garden Club Detective." Bob explained that the picture in the middle was supposed to be some delphiniums.

I see Cora Medford most Sundays and know most of Pauline Giesley's story. In fact, we get it repeated every week. So I had figured it was about time that I did visit Viola Coleport. But I had not figured out how to really do that until I got my new position. The Buena Vista Garden Club, you see, is part of

Viola's heritage and includes several of her close friends.

After checking that Viola would be in, I got Mary Lizabeth to drive me over to Blanchard Hills Drive. Mary Lizabeth can be shy at times. Oh yes, she can hold her own down at the Cup and Saucer, but she does not feel comfortable out among "society" types. I tell her they are people just like the rest of us. "I'd prefer to hear about them than have them lookin' at me," she says. At any rate once I was deposited at Viola's, she announced that she would run some errands for an hour or so.

Viola's house was built when it was unfashionable to have more than one floor. They put in enough care that it still looks respectable even by more recent standards, but it does seem to sprawl. There are tall trees on either side, and some between the house and the street. The back or south side is open, and that is where the garden is. Nowadays, you have to have your swimming pool back there, too.

Viola guided me into her living room and to a comfortable armchair. She pulled up another for herself.

"Would you like some iced tea, Mrs. Bushrow?"

She had a glass pitcher on a table near our chairs, and when I indicated I would have a glass, she poured us each one. It was one of these new raspberry concoctions and just hit the spot for a summer's evening.

"Viola, I am so sorry about your sister. It must be especially hard on you with all the police investigation and so on."

"I am so glad the club got you to look into all of this. Don Cochran is just flailing away at everything and everybody. I had my troubles before, but they seem minor compared to what's occurred. I don't think anyone can sleep easily until we really find out what happened to Rita."

I shook my head slightly. Viola did seem to be in a bind.

"It must be awful. Have you heard anything from George Claymore or Geof?"

"Yes, they called me. It seems the sheriff out there has been asking them questions. Both of them were in Texas on June 6. To tell you the truth, George was the least unhappy of us all to hear that Rita had died. They had gone through some rough times. All the same, he was shocked at how it happened. Geof was a little bit upset. All these questions have not helped his condition."

By "condition," Viola meant his paranoia.

"I understand that you had your own rough time with Rita just before she left for Knoxville."

Viola told me about the episode that appears in Don Cochran's report.

"I am sure it was Betty Marie Grumberry who heard us go at each other that Monday," she concluded. "She has always been the nosy type."

"Did you say 'Monday'?"

"Yes, I figured out that it was that Monday."

"Don Cochran seems to think it was on Wednesday at three o'clock."

"He *would* get it mixed up. It was Monday,

because before I went over to Rita's, I picked up the sunglasses I left at church the day before. Come to think of it, I know where I was on Wednesday, too. I was picking up some flowers at Charlie Gunn's floral shop. His assistant didn't know what Rita had ordered, so I had to wait until he came back at three."

"You were getting some flowers for Rita?"

"Oh, I know it seems strange after the mutual eruption we had had two days before, but she was my sister. Anyway, Rita always had that ability to get you to do things even when you didn't want to. That's how she was able to get all the things she was involved with to happen. She needed several things for the Knoxville show but didn't have the time to get them. She gave me her credit card and told me to head downtown."

I asked if she had kept the receipt.

"No, I think I gave all that to Rita when I gave the card back. In fact, I don't remember seeing it when I went through her desk. That is one thing I will look for over at Rita's. I am going to have to tell Geof about this. He will appreciate the police making such a mistake."

That was all very interesting. We talked on about the McDurries until Mary Lizabeth returned for me. Viola saw me out to the car. She was smiling slightly. I would too if I had just found out that I had an alibi for a murder.

The next morning I called Charles Gunn's shop.

"This is Mrs. Lamar Bushrow."

"Well, hello, Mrs. Bushrow. It is good to hear from you again."

Charlie had been part of the Randy Hartwell crowd involved in *The Historical Society Murder Mystery*.

"I am afraid I have connected you to another murder, if ever so slightly."

"Considering how you kept me out of trouble on the last one, I don't think I have too much to worry about. How can I help you?"

"Do you remember Viola Coleport coming into your shop the week before Rita Claymore died?"

"Yes, I do. She was buying flowers for her sister."

"Could you tell me which day that was?"

"That's a little harder to recall. I know it wasn't the day before she was killed."

"Do you have the credit card records still? Viola says she used her sister's card."

"Let me get back to you on that one. Normally I wouldn't give that information out, but you are one of the folks in the white hats."

Charlie called me back after a few minutes.

"Yes, Viola Coleport bought some kan-paws at 3:07 P.M. on June 3. She was using Rita Claymore's card. I normally wouldn't let anyone use someone else's card, but I knew both of them, and Mrs. Claymore was a good customer."

So you see, someone else was in the garden arguing with Rita about money.

Reward Offered in Murder Case

Mrs. Irvine Coleport is now offering a reward of $5,000 for information leading to the arrest and successful prosecution of the murderer of her late sister, Marguerite Claymore.

"As no one has stepped forward to identify the person who did this thing, I am hoping that our money will prod someone to come forward," Mrs. Coleport said. "This is not just about my sister, but about our community."

Although the particulars of Mrs. Claymore's estate are still being worked out, Judge Legget of the Probate Court granted Mrs. Coleport's petition that funds be set aside for the reward.

Up to this point the investigation has been characterized by delays and false leads. One suspect was arrested and then later released.

Asked about the reward, Lt. Don Cochran said he welcomed the help, but doubted that this would solve the mystery overnight. "Continued diligence by law enforcement agencies will be what concludes this investigation," he stated.

XXIV

Bits and Bytes

SLATER WATTS

Here is Slater Watts with my second report. For your eyes only!

My folks have always been about helping other people out. It's our duty. My great-grandfather Watts came to Borderville with the railroad. He was a conductor. Even my father served in the army in Vietnam. Once we see something needs to be done, we get right to it.

There is no surprise I would help find who got Mrs. Claymore. I used to do her yard, and I felt like I ought to do something for her.

My mother let me into the high school computer lab.

Jeremy Stritt had given me two floppy disks with screen savers. I copied these onto two other disks. Those disks with the Eureka Screen Saver labels were going to be used for something else. I put just one real screen saver on each disk and created several more dummy ones to "fill" the directories. I even came up with some "install" files so that it would actually work. To put the icing on the cake, each disk got a hidden directory.

This was going to be smooth! If someone looked at these things after I got the data, he would only see store-bought stuff.

Thursday night it was off to the True Path Church.

We started with all the brothers brought together. We sang songs I was not used to like "I Can Believe in Myself" and "You Have to Grab the Gold at the End of the Rainbow."

Rob Davis and Jerry Glasgow sat next to me at supper. I asked them if anyone at ICD had gotten to Ninth Order.

Rob said, "I bet Mike Shirk did. He did something last month and got to go someplace, so I guess he got Ninth Order. We may be a new division, but I'll bet we'll have lots of brothers get there."

Jerry said, "You're not supposed to tell anyone below your order what you see."

Rob explained some more. "Yeah, Mike is original ICD stuff. He and the Reverend talked a lot."

"What are the other divisions?" I asked.

"Oh, you can't tell a First Order brother that," said Jerry.

After supper, I got put in front of the computer. Jon Sidan gave me a list of contributors and the amounts they had contributed. They were things like "Mr. Charles Larken $234.67 July 14." Everything was printed out neatly. The top of the page said: "Contributions ICD."

"Is this the only computer you've got?" I asked Jon.

"We also have one in the basement."

So that was it. They must have printed this one out from the other one; but man, it would still have been easier to do everything on one machine.

I also got some disks for backing up the database. Jon showed me how to do this. He didn't know what Slater Watts, Secret Agent, was going to do with *that*.

I started entering the contribution stuff. All of these people had already given before, so I didn't need to enter their addresses. After a while Jon walked down the hall to talk with Reverend Boheem.

I crossed the room and pulled out my super-duper supposedly screen saver disks from my backpack. Oh, they looked sweet! I put the first one in and started loading files.

The database was stored on four files: "Addresses.dat," "Contacts.dat," "Contrib1.dat," and "Contrib2.dat." I was pleased to get them all on the two disks.

At that point I heard Jon Sidan coming back down the hall, and dang it, I didn't have time to get the disks into my backpack. I pulled the second disk out of the floppy drive and put both of them next to the regular backup disks.

"How's it going?" Jon asked.

He was leaning over my shoulder.

"Okay," I replied.

"Hey, what's this?"

He had spotted the super-duper disks.

I heard myself say to myself, Be calm. We can still get through this.

"Those are some screen saver disks," I said.

It sounded pretty calm. So far so good. I managed to type another line of contributions.

Jon picked up the first disk and read from the label, "To put these Eureka Screen Savers on your system, put Disk 1 in your floppy drive and type 'a:\install' at the DOS prompt."

"Yeah," I said, "someone gave me those, but I don't have a computer. I thought maybe I could try them out here."

"We didn't get any screen savers with this computer."

I bet you just have that option turned off, I thought to myself.

"It would be great to have some. Here, let me try," Jon said.

I got up. Jon sat in my chair and inserted Disk 1. My heart leaped to my throat as he clicked on the File Manager and displayed the contents of the disk. I knew I was in the lions' den now. But he couldn't see the hidden directory.

He clicked on the install.bat file. It was showtime, and I was facing the lions head-on.

I had things set up so that the computer would copy and then delete the one good screen saver several times before leaving a copy on the machine. It made it look like it was transferring more than one file. Then it would ask for the second disk.

Jon put in the second disk as I silently prayed: "Oh Lord, please make this work. Next time I won't try to be so fancy. I'll just do the basic job."

The computer finished its copying.

"Now, how do we see what we've got?" Jon asked.

"Let's see," I said. "Just let me sit down."

I opened up the screen-settings program. Sure enough, these folks didn't have their screen saver option set. I clicked that check box and went down the list of installed screen savers. Right there among all the other ones were the two from the disks. It had worked! I selected the one called "Tall Ships" and clicked the "test" button. The screen went blue, and sailboats started going across it.

"Hey, I like that," Jon said.

You have no idea how relieved I was. I put the screen saver disks in my backpack and finished typing in the contributors. Reverend Boheem came by.

"You've got to see this," Jon said. "Slater, show Reverend Boheem what we've done. Show him the sea thing."

I realized I was not as relieved as I thought.

"Okay. Just wait a little while, and it will pop up."

I had already shut down the database and was getting ready to leave. I knew if I ran off now, they might suspect something and set the hounds after me. We waited one-and-one-half eternities until the ships showed up on the computer.

"That is superb, Slater." Reverend Boheem can be oh so warm when he wants to be. "We will have to get one of the Nile next."

I figured I could escape into the night, and I did.

XXV

The Tangled Web

BOB KELSEY

Slater arrived on Friday morning with a big grin. He had two floppy disks with him.

"Mr. Kelsey, I think I've got what we wanted. I'm going to get my mom to let me use one of the school's computers this afternoon. We're going to have this *all* figured out."

I had some hedges to trim, and Slater reported to them on the previous night's events. He got through quickly enough that I could let him leave early.

The next day, Slater came back.

"Can I use your computer, Mr. Kelsey?"

"Sure."

I had gotten a computer several years ago. I had thought I could keep our finances and Leota could record her cooking recipes on the thing. It has turned out to be a glorified typewriter.

For Slater, it was something more. He wouldn't let me in the den while he worked the thing—he didn't want another "soul" around—but I could tell that he made it sing. It wasn't long before he came into the kitchen where I was reading the paper.

"Could I read the funnies, please?"

"Certainly, Slater."

I handed him that section.

"Oh, by the way, Mr. Kelsey, I think I left

something in your printer. Could you please get it for me?"

He said this with a big grin and a wink.

When I got to the den, I found several sheets of paper still in the printer. The first was the following list:

Contrib2.dat

Donaldson	$1265.00
Barnwell	$1623.00
Brinker	$2121.00
Claymore	$234.00
Dangerfield	$1819.00
Douglas	$932.00
Duffy	$1156.00
Epperson	$2944.00
Frothmore	$456.00
Harmon	$1345.00
Hedgecox	$870.00
Larken	$900.00
Osterman	$56.00
Peterson	$328.00
Simmons	$2469.00
Sudberry	$3198.00
Vernon	$980.00

I figured that this was the list of contributors Slater was working with on Thursday night. My first reaction was that the folks who had been robbed must be giving to Reverend Boheem so that the crime wave could be stopped, but then I noticed the strange totals for the donations. Normally when someone gives to a charity in these amounts, that person writes out checks in multiples of $5.

These numbers could not come from a combination of such gifts.

Then I noticed Rita's name.

Rita Claymore I don't think would have been somebody to give to ICD—at least not before she got robbed. She was one for running things before giving an outfit money. I also doubted if Viola Coleport would have been able to give on behalf of her sister, either.

Were these records of the "take" on each crime? If so, why would Boheem let someone new like Slater enter all this stuff into the computer?

The second list was titled "Contacts.dat." Most of the names were from out of town, but I recognized one from Borderville: Camille Hythorp. What did she have to do with all this?

I went back to the kitchen and handed Slater the lists.

"Have you ever been to Boudoir City, Louisiana, or Richport, Missouri, or Kiute, Arizona, Mr. Kelsey?"

No, I hadn't. I recognized these towns as some of the ones for the contacts.

"Well, I went surfing on the World Wide Web yesterday to see what those places are like. Boudoir City has a casino. Richport has a floating casino, and Kiute has a *big* ol' casino. The same thing goes for Wigwam, Connecticut, and Chupahee, New Mexico."

That would explain about half of the names on that list. The others were major cities like New York, Boston, and Philadelphia. It certainly gave us something to mull over.

"Slater, you have been doing some very

good work recently. Why don't you take it easy for a while? You should probably just go with the flow."

"Actually I was going to go fishing today. Thank you for letting me use your computer."

"Any time."

I watched Slater leave on his bicycle. He had his fishing rod with him.

XXVI

In the Rose Garden

HARRIET BUSHROW

I knew Slater Watts was made of the right ingredients. Of course, he has the right kind of family, and that counts for a lot. The way he could go into that ICD and get all that information was something else. Bob Kelsey came over one afternoon and showed me what Slater had gotten from the computer. It amazes me you can get *anything* out of those gizmos, let alone the stuff you want.

So, Camille Hythorp was involved in all this. I realized it was time to find out what she knew.

The two Bordervilles—Virginia and Tennessee—share one public library. Several years ago, an addition was put on the original building, creating a small courtyard between the old and new parts. It had been a dreary little place until Rita Claymore decided the Buena Vista Garden Club should do something about it. But now it has a curved brick walk and a pleasant gurgling fountain. On the sunny side is a collection of roses.

It really is quite attractive.

Every Tuesday morning during the summer, Camille comes down to tend to the roses. I knew if I got there, I could probably talk to her while she made sure the bushes were in good shape.

It really is too bad I can't drive any more. Not only do I have to figure out who did

166

these murders, but I have to figure out a way to get around to see what is going on. Fortunately, Bob Kelsey was oh so gracious in taking me down to the library. You can tell his mother raised him properly.

While I hobbled into the courtyard, Bob took a seat in the magazine section near one of the windows. If I can't make grand entrances any more, at least I can be centerstage when the curtain goes up. I was able to seat myself on a bench against one end of the space. A trellis arches over the bench so that you can't see the spot from the side. And the fountain blocks it from being seen from the opposite end. But when the sunlight comes in later in the day, it makes a pleasant nook for reading.

The Garden Club had the trellis painted a dark green and a white rose planted on one side and a red one on the other. The two bushes had grown to the extent that each had reached over the arch. The intermingling of the two hues made a spectacular sight. I have had worse places to do my detective work.

Eventually the door opened and Camille stepped in. She was wearing her work clothes and carried a bucket with her tools.

"Hello, Camille."

"Hello, Mrs. Bushrow."

"I need to talk with you."

"Oh?"

"Yes. Why don't you sit down by me here?"

Camille set down her bucket and sat down on the bench beside me.

"The police are figuring out that Alec

Boheem has been orchestrating all these robberies, including the one at Rita's place."

Camille sat silent, scarcely breathing.

"When they finally get him, I am afraid they are going to find your name as one of their contacts."

My companion might as well have become part of the garden statuary.

"The day before the Knoxville show, someone had an argument with Rita over money. You're the treasurer for the Buena Vista Club. Camille; was that you?"

She just looked down at the ground.

"Could it have something to do with casino gambling?"

Camille began to stir.

I continued, "You can either throw in your lot with Don Cochran, or you can have it all out right here."

"Yes," she said finally. "It has something to do with casino gambling. I have been out of control for some time now. I think I have always been impulsive, but the past couple of years have been hell. Hell."

She paused to catch her breath, then continued:

"I was generally able to take care of myself after Don died, but one day, on a whim, I decided to get a lottery ticket. I can remember when preachers talked about how terrible horse racing was. A lottery ticket seemed like a different thing. It appeared to be 'official' and controlled. It was supposed to be just for entertainment.

"Well, I enjoyed buying the tickets. Early

on, I won some money. Looking back on it, I now realize that I was buying a lot of those things. No one I knew really went in for that kind of thing, so I didn't admit to myself that I was falling into a trap.

"Then I decided to go see Branson, Missouri, with a friend. On the way, we stayed in Richport because they can subsidize the hotel rooms from their casino proceeds. I decided I would go see the casino. Before I knew it, it was morning, but I was ahead with the money.

"I was hooked at that point. When I had to sell some stock to pay for the new roof, I sold some extra so I could go to the slot machines. I didn't do so well this time. Since I didn't have the dividends from that stock any more, I had to sell some more when I needed a new car. There was some of that money set aside for the casino.

"I realized I needed to recoup my losses. A substantial payoff meant substantial bets, I thought. Eventually, I decided to sell all of my furnishings. It made me feel like I was finally getting down to business. This would be the one that would see me through, I thought.

"I lost it all. At the time, I was in the bar at the casino in Kiute, Arizona. Reality had set in. I was actually crying. That's when Alec Boheem walked up."

Camille stopped at this point. I sensed that she had only done Act I of her story.

After a few moments of silence, I asked, "This garden was your idea, wasn't it?"

Camille gazed at the fountain.

"That is true."

"And Rita took all the credit?"

"That is also true. Rita wanted to put all the effort into the beds in the front. I realized this little courtyard would get so much more attention, and it would be easier to maintain with fewer people walking through here. When it was all finished, Rita was the one who got her picture in the paper."

That certainly fit Rita to a T.

Camille sighed and looked over at the fountain again.

"I think you *do* understand," she finally said.

I put on my best reassuring face and nodded my head.

"Alec Boheem also understood," she went on. "Oh, I think I was very transparent sitting there in that bar. He came up to me and asked what was wrong. He has those eyes that mesmerize, and so I told him everything.

"He explained that he was some kind of pastor and that he had a special mission fund for people who spent all their money gambling. Before I knew it, he produced a check covering all the losses of my trip. I was so overwhelmed at becoming a 'charity case,' I didn't consider where the money was coming from.

"I told him I didn't know how I would ever repay him. I found out, though. A couple of days after I returned to Borderville, Alec gave me a call. He was interested in starting a mission in Borderville and asked if I would be willing to sit on his board of advisers. I really couldn't say no.

"Alec arrived about a year and a half ago. Every once in a while I would get a call for some piece of information. I told ICD—that's what the group was called—how the schools were set up, who would contribute to help juvenile delinquents, and other such matters.

"Then he started asking particulars about some of the people. Did the Barnwells have a computer? Were the Eppersons into hunting? I told him what I knew, but I realized something was up when these people started getting robbed.

"When he called the next time, I refused to give him any more information. 'Camille,' he said, oh so cooly, 'don't you realize that you are up to your chin in this already? How do you think I was able to pay off your gambling debts?'

"The creep then explained how the game was going to be played. I would be his informant and add legitimacy to his operation; in return, I would get payments. There would be nowhere to hide as his organization would be able to find me anywhere."

"What is this group like?" I asked.

"You see Alec Boheem is part of a gypsy network set up to go after towns like ours. While they let the more established crime groups run the gambling centers, they use the casinos to find people like me to be their contacts. Once an operation is established, young hoodlums are trained to do the break-ins. The adolescents are less likely to get put in jail if they are caught and are more loyal. All the cer-

171

emonies are based on Egypt because the Gypsies are supposed to have come from there originally, although I think they really come from Central Europe. I guess Egypt is a little more exotic."

"Camille, you must tell me: how did Rita get targeted?"

"ICD finds out about people through the newspaper. The boys go through the pages every day with an eye to what may be stolen and when would be a good time to make an attack. The publicity over the Garden Gala made Rita a target, but there is more to it than that.

"Not too long after I realized what was going on, Alec Boheem brought me a payment. I had several bills I needed to address, and like a fool, I accepted the money. Instead of taking care of the bills, I took a trip to a casino where I gambled it all away. I knew then how much I was on a leash.

"That's also how the flap with Rita came about. I'm the treasurer for the club, as you pointed out. Although I was broke, I happened to have the club checkbook with me and remembered that there was two hundred dollars in the account. Alec had told me I would be given more money shortly, so I cashed in one of the club's checks. I was able to repay the amount after about a week.

"But Rita got ahold of the bank statement before I did and zeroed in on this check. The day before we left for Knoxville, she called me over to her house. I had not really thought through what I had done, and so I confessed how I had used the money. She was furious, but she wasn't going to do anything to me until after the gala. She just needed me to be an ornament in her crown.

"The first night down in Knoxville, I called back up here to Borderville to get the messages off my answering machine. One of them was from Alec Boheem, asking me to call him. It's amazing how if you were brought up in a certain way, you have to return someone's call even if he is a thief. I returned his call.

"He wanted to know if Pauline Giesley had any silver and where she might keep it. I of course had just seen how she had been disqualified."

Camille quoted me the conversation:

"Don't bother Pauline," Camille said. "Rita has been giving her a hard time."

"Rita Claymore?" Boheem responded.

"Yes, Rita Claymore."

"I bet she has some silver."

All Camille could think of was the way Pauline had been treated and then that big punch bowl.

"Yes, she has silver."

"Where does she keep it?"

"In her dining room, I believe."

Camille returned to our present discussion. With slightly more effort, she said, "So you see, I initiated the attack on Rita. If I had not had that conversation, Rita would still be alive."

Up to this point, Camille had been sort of leaning toward me. Now she sat up slightly straighter. She was relieved to have gotten through all that without me raking her over the coals, but I could see her eyes welling up with tears.

"Camille, who was the actual person who did the break-in?"

"It was one of Alec's boys. They've sent him off someplace."

So, the death had been part of her robbery, after all. The boy had set out just to take the silver and ended up taking Rita to her grave. And Camille didn't know what she was getting herself into when she started buying lottery tickets. All these folks had found their actions blossoming into more than they'd bargained.

"Mrs. Bushrow, what am I going to do?"

It was something to consider. By this point, Camille was crying.

"This is certainly a mess," I said, as I shook my head sympathetically. "For right now, you can sit tight. Don Cochran is going to have to see that you have a connection to Boheem. You may very well have to tell him what has happened, but he will be more interested in nabbing the person who has been orchestrating all of this."

The poor woman and I sat there for a while. She did look pitiful but not completely despondent.

Then I said that I really had to be going. "Thank you for that remarkable story."

By this time the sun had reached our bench. I left Camille still contemplating her situation and doddered back into the building. That sweet Bob Kelsey was sitting patiently reading a news magazine, but he perked up as soon as I started telling him what I had learned.

New Arrests in Claymore Case

Lt. Don Cochran announced today that he has made several arrests that relate not only to the death of Mrs. Marguerite Claymore but also to the recent rash of robberies.

Rev. Alexander Boheem, Pastor of the Golden Rule Congregation of the True Path Church, and his assistant, Jonathan Sidan, were apprehended yesterday afternoon.

The two are each being charged with 17 counts of robbery and one of murder.

Lt. Cochran also indicated that a juvenile had been detained in Chupahee, New Mexico in conjunction with the case. In accordance with police department policy, this person's name will not be released.

The two Borderville men are alleged to be the masterminds behind a robbery ring primarily responsible for the break-ins of the last several months. This group, the Order of the Isis Command Division, ostensibly was intended to reform juvenile delinquents but instead further trained them in crime.

Rev. Debra Mollusk, Assistant Pastor of the Corinth Street United Methodist Church, found the arrests to be politically motivated. "This is payback for the protest Alec [Boheem] held down at the City Council. It's the kind of problem you have with male patriarchal systems."

"I expect that our community will be much safer after these actions," said Lt. Cochran.

XXVII

The End of It All

BOB KELSEY

I must say, it was wonderful how Harriet Bushrow got Camille Hythorp to tell her side of the story. Of course, it was all going to have to come out somehow. I guess Camille thought she had better odds with Harriet than with Don Cochran.

As I drove Harriet back to her house that day, she was in a reflective mood.

"You know, Bob, we get into one of these things and hone in on the mystery. When that's all figured out, we are left with the people."

She then proceeded to tell me what she had learned in the courtyard. At the end, her eyes began to twinkle.

"I imagine Don Cochran will be as pleased as punch to learn the murder really *was* connected to the robbery," she said.

It seems everything and everybody was connected to the murder or its solution. If Pauline Giesley had not gotten disqualified, she would have been the one who got robbed; and there might not have been a murder at all. Don Cochran's interrogation of Laura Gooding prompted the Garden Club to appoint Harriet Bushrow as official detective. As official detective, Harriet got to see Viola Coleport.

Slater got to be both a suspect and a detective.

I turned the files Slater had sneaked out of ICD over to Lieutenant Cochran and explained the connection to the casino towns. I further suggested that he try and find Mike Shirk at one of those towns.

Sure enough, Shirk was found somewhere in Chupahee, New Mexico. He had been the intruder who attacked Rita Claymore and was very upset with what he had done. Boheem had sent him out west to settle down and not cause any more trouble. When the police out there located him, he was willing to tell everything about Boheem. That's what led to those arrests you may have read about in the paper.

Boheem was fairly skilled at keeping people from betraying his operation. He usually got someone well involved before that someone realized he was doing something illegal, and—as in Camille Hythorp's case—he used that accomplice status to enforce loyalty. Slater was allowed to work on those sensitive files because it would get his hands dirty with the seemingly innocent databases.

Shirk revealed just how ambitious ICD was. Boheem was planning on expanding to another city and leaving Jon Sidan to run the Borderville operation; thus ours was Isis Command Division I. This explains the shape of that pin we found in Rita's garden.

In Camille Hythorp's case, when Don Cochran asked why her name was in the list of contacts, she just said she was on the board for the Circle of ICD, which did not know what was really going on with the organization. After some questions about some of the board meetings, Lieutenant Cochran seemed satisfied. Camille says the whole episode has scared her out of her wits, and she is starting to put her financial situation in order.

Slater Watts got the reward that Viola Coleport was offering. He is using it to buy a computer. He is also looking into getting a car. Charlotte Wisp has hired him again: she now considers him a hero.

Dr. McDavit from the First Presbyterian Church is working with the remaining ICD kids. He intends to show them that a church is a place of openness and light, and more important, healing.

As for Harriet Bushrow, she is enjoying all the publicity. She just carries on. There will be none like her when she leaves this world.